OTTO'S
BACKWARDS DAY

A TOON BOOK BY

FRANK CAMMUSO
with JAY LYNCH

A JUNIOR LIBRARY GUILD SELECTION

Also look for Otto's Orange Day, by the same authors.

For Khai

Editorial Director: FRANÇOISE MOULY

Book Design: FRANÇOISE MOULY & JONATHAN BENNETT

FRANK CAMMUSO'S artwork was drawn in india ink and colored digitally.

A TOON Book™ © 2013 RAW Junior, LLC, 27 Greene Street, New York, NY 10013. TOON Books®, TOON Graphics™, LITTLE LIT® and TOON Into Reading™ are trademarks of RAW Junior, LLC. All rights reserved. No part of this book may be used or reproduced in any manner whatsoever without written permission except in the case of brief quotations embodied in critical articles and reviews. All our books are Smyth Sewn (the highest library-quality binding available) and printed with soy-based inks on acid-free woodfree paper harvested from responsible sources. Printed in China by C&C Offset Printing Co., Ltd. Distributed to the trade by Consortium Book Sales and Distribution, Inc.; orders (800) 283-3572; orderentry@perseusbooks.com; www.cbsd.com.

The Library of Congress has cataloged the hardcover edition as follows:

Otto's backwards day : a TOON book / by Frank Cammuso with Jay Lynch.

   pages cm. -- (Easy-to-read comics. Level 3)

Summary: "Someone stole Otto's birthday! When Otto the cat and his robot sidekick Toot follow the crook, they discover a topsy-turvy world where rats chase cats and people wear underpants over their clothes"-- Provided by publisher.

ISBN 978-1-935179-33-7 (alk. paper)

1. Graphic novels. [1. Graphic novels. 2. Birthdays--Fiction. 3. Cats--Fiction. 4. Humorous stories.] I. Lynch, Jay, author. II. Title.

PZ7.7.C36Or 2013   741.5'973--dc23   2012047661

   ISBN: 978-1-935179-33-7 (hardcover)   ISBN: 978-1-943145-33-1 (paperback)

   17 18 19 20 21 22 C&C 10 9 8 7 6 5 4 3 2 1

WWW.TOON-BOOKS.COM

CHAPTER ONE

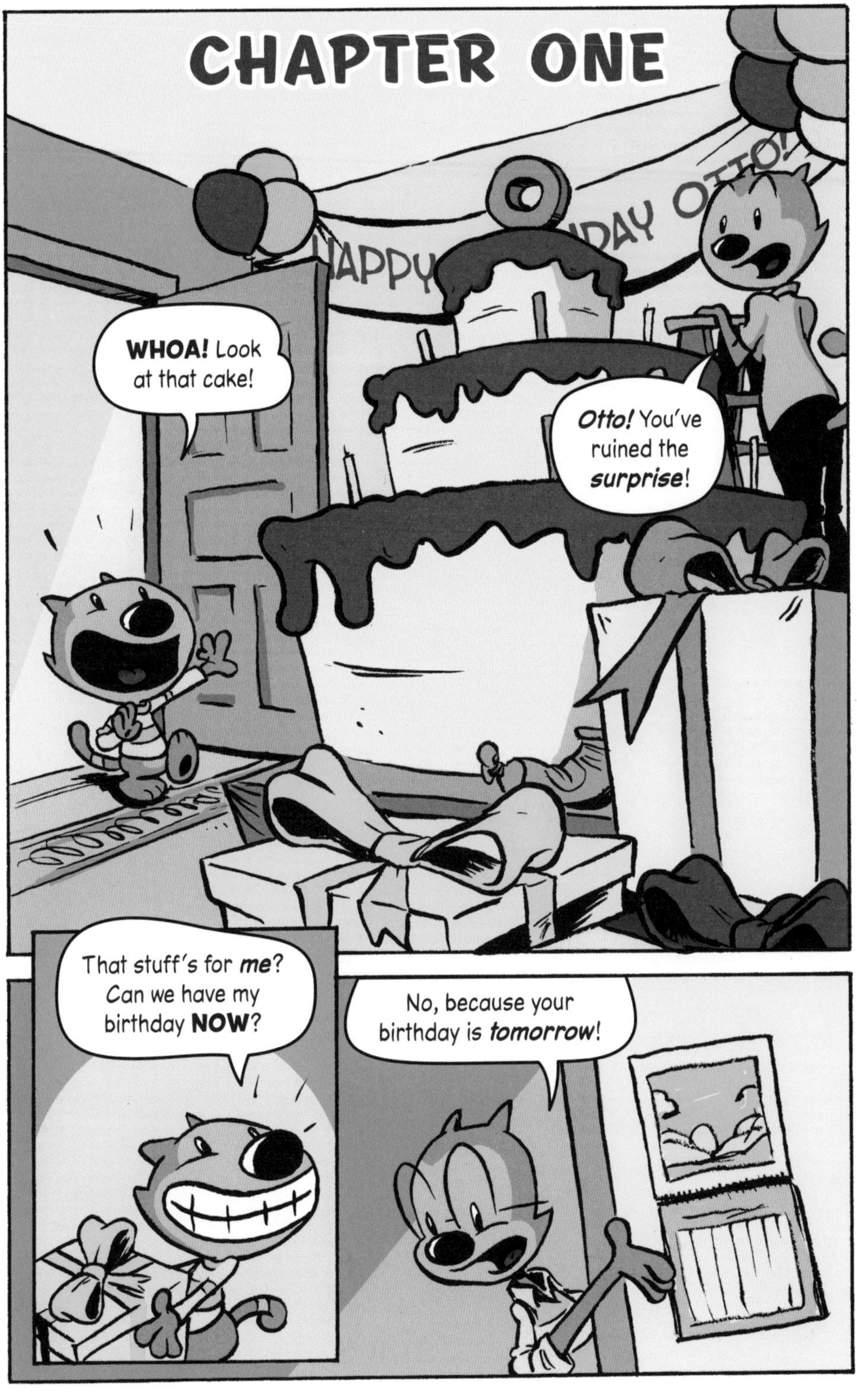
WHOA! Look at that cake!
Otto! You've ruined the ***surprise***!
That stuff's for ***me***? Can we have my birthday **NOW**?
No, because your birthday is ***tomorrow***!

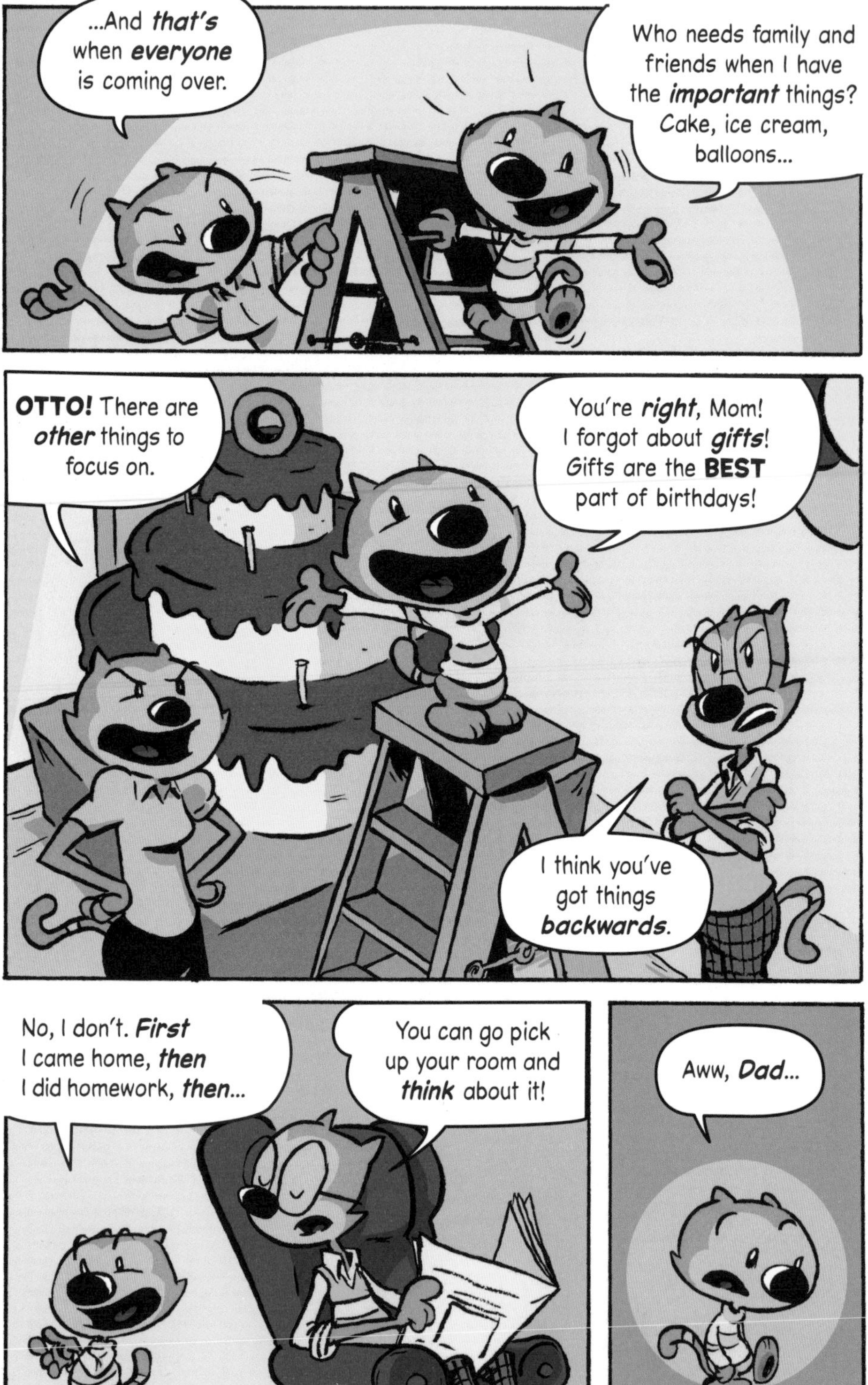

...And *that's* when *everyone* is coming over.
Who needs family and friends when I have the *important* things? Cake, ice cream, balloons...
OTTO! There are *other* things to focus on.
You're *right*, Mom! I forgot about *gifts*! Gifts are the **BEST** part of birthdays!
I think you've got things *backwards*.
No, I don't. *First* I came home, *then* I did homework, *then*...
You can go pick up your room and *think* about it!
Aww, *Dad*...

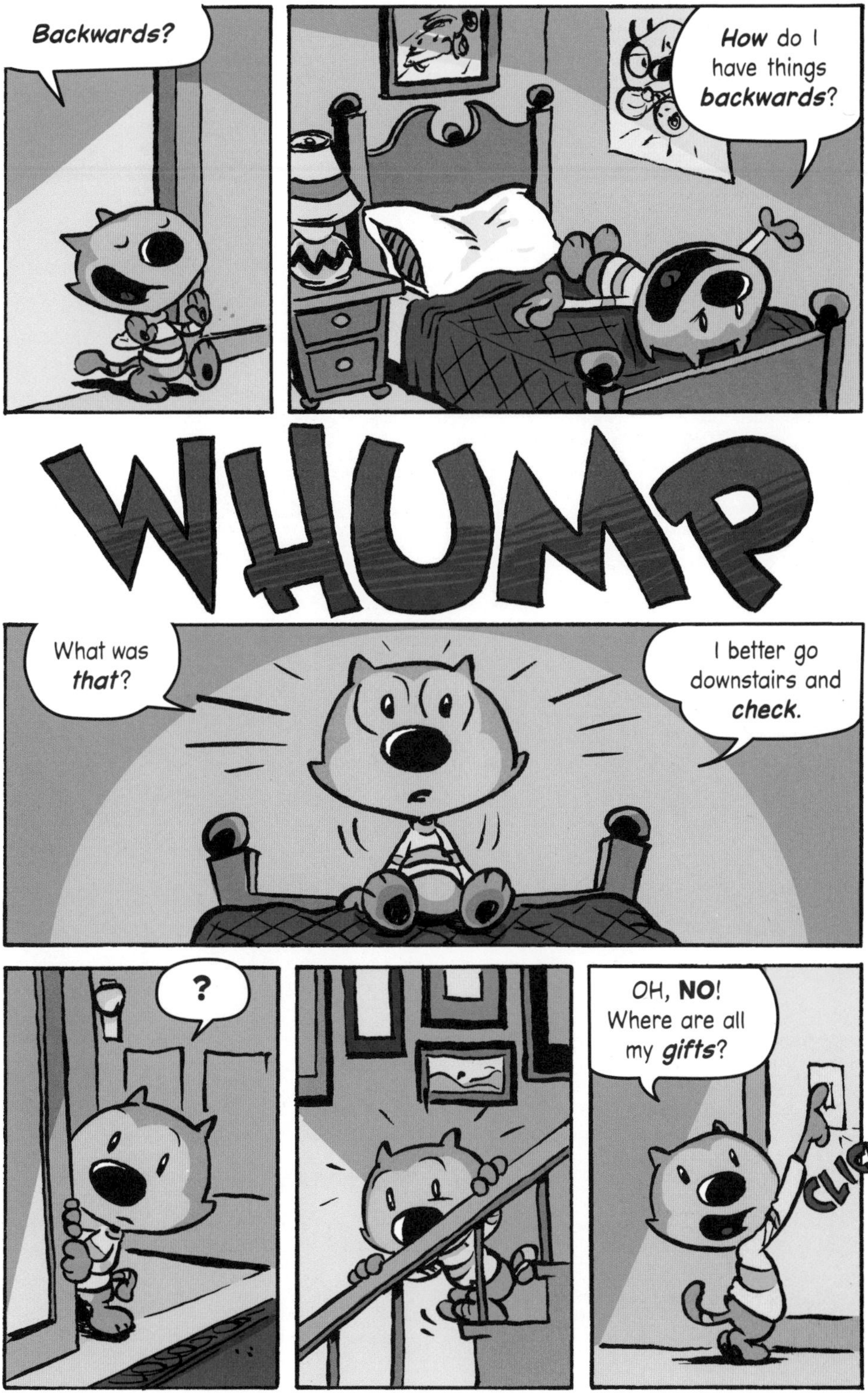

Backwards?
How do I have things backwards?
WHUMP
What was that?
I better go downstairs and check.
?
OH, NO! Where are all my gifts?
CLICK

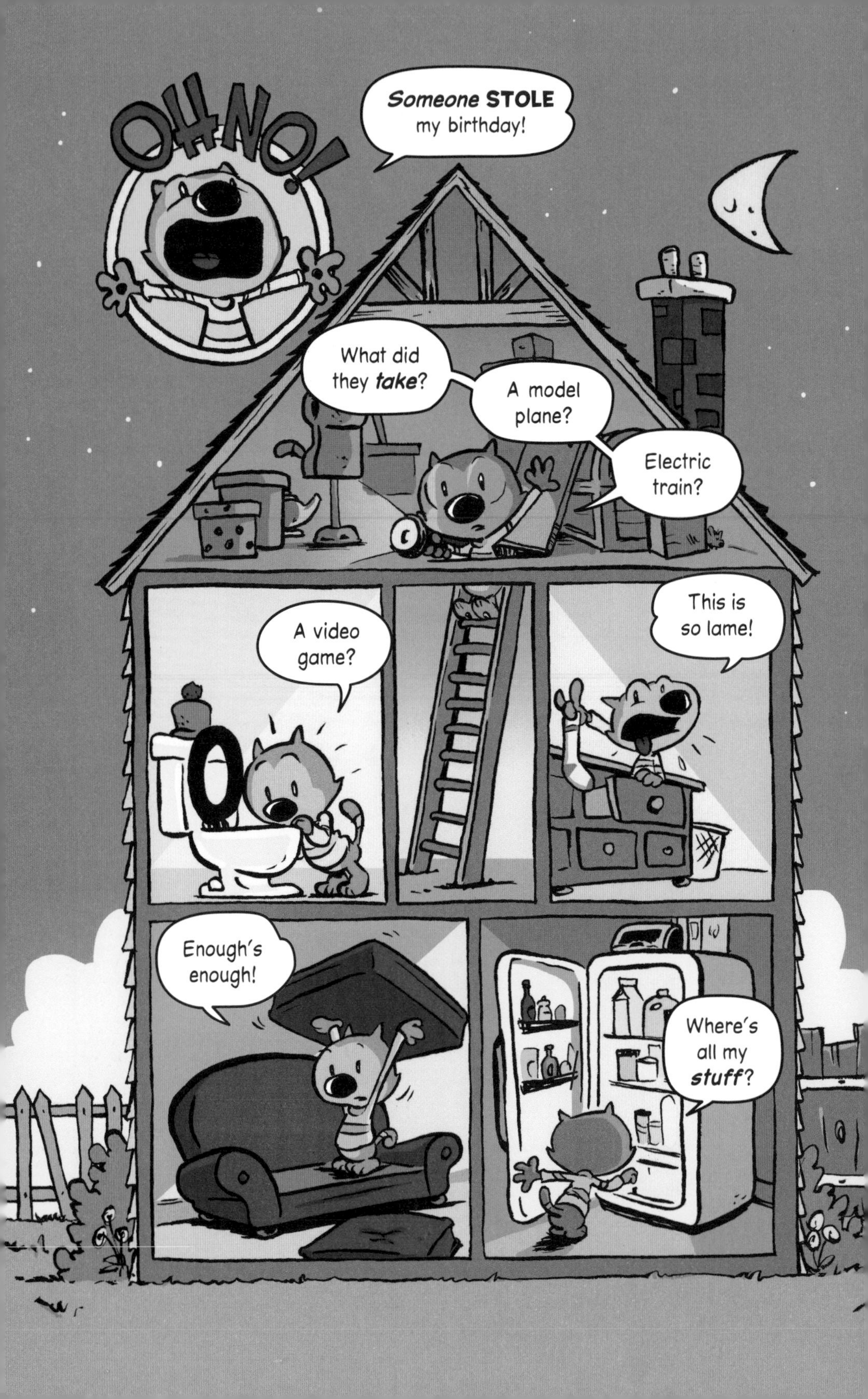
OH NO!
Someone **STOLE** my birthday!
What did they ***take***?
A model plane?
Electric train?
A video game?
This is so lame!
Enough's enough!
Where's all my ***stuff***?

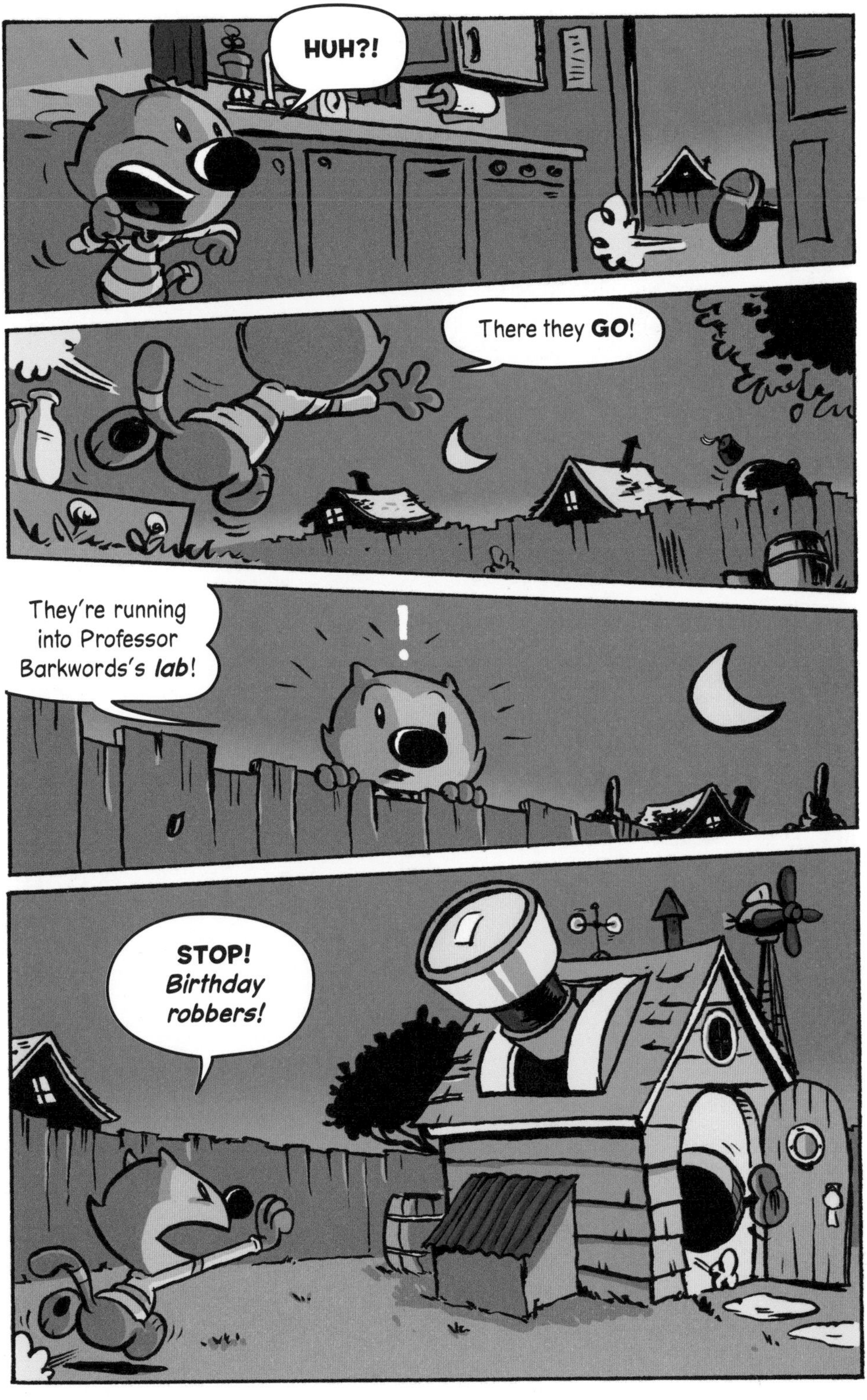
HUH?!
There they **GO**!
They're running into Professor Barkwords's ***lab***!
!
STOP!
Birthday robbers!

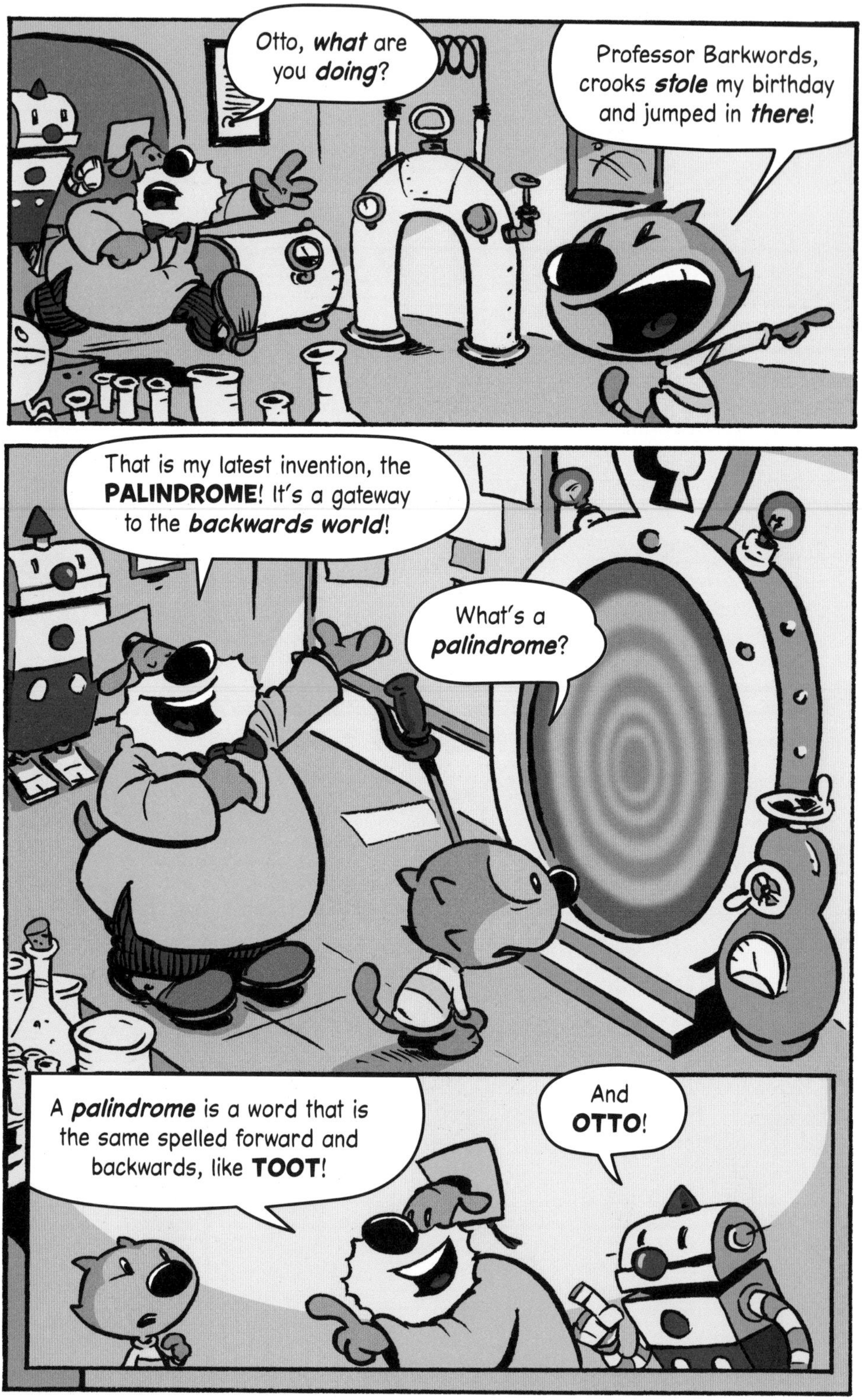
Otto, *what* are you *doing*?
Professor Barkwords, crooks *stole* my birthday and jumped in *there*!
That is my latest invention, the **PALINDROME**! It's a gateway to the *backwards world*!
What's a *palindrome*?
A *palindrome* is a word that is the same spelled forward and backwards, like **TOOT**!
And **OTTO**!

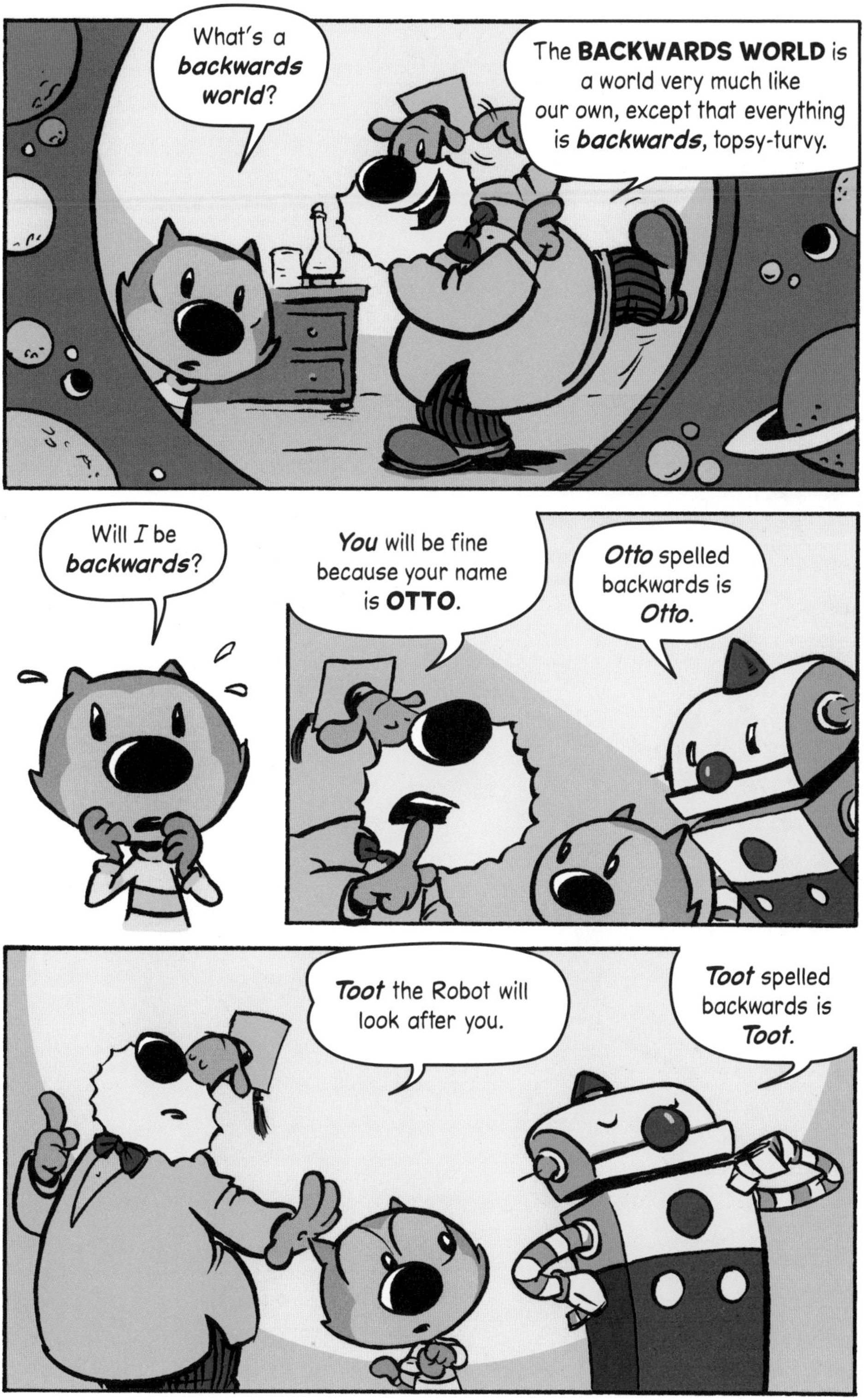
What's a *backwards world*?
The **BACKWARDS WORLD** is a world very much like our own, except that everything is ***backwards***, topsy-turvy.
Will *I* be ***backwards***?
You will be fine because your name is **OTTO**.
Otto spelled backwards is ***Otto***.
Toot the Robot will look after you.
Toot spelled backwards is ***Toot***.

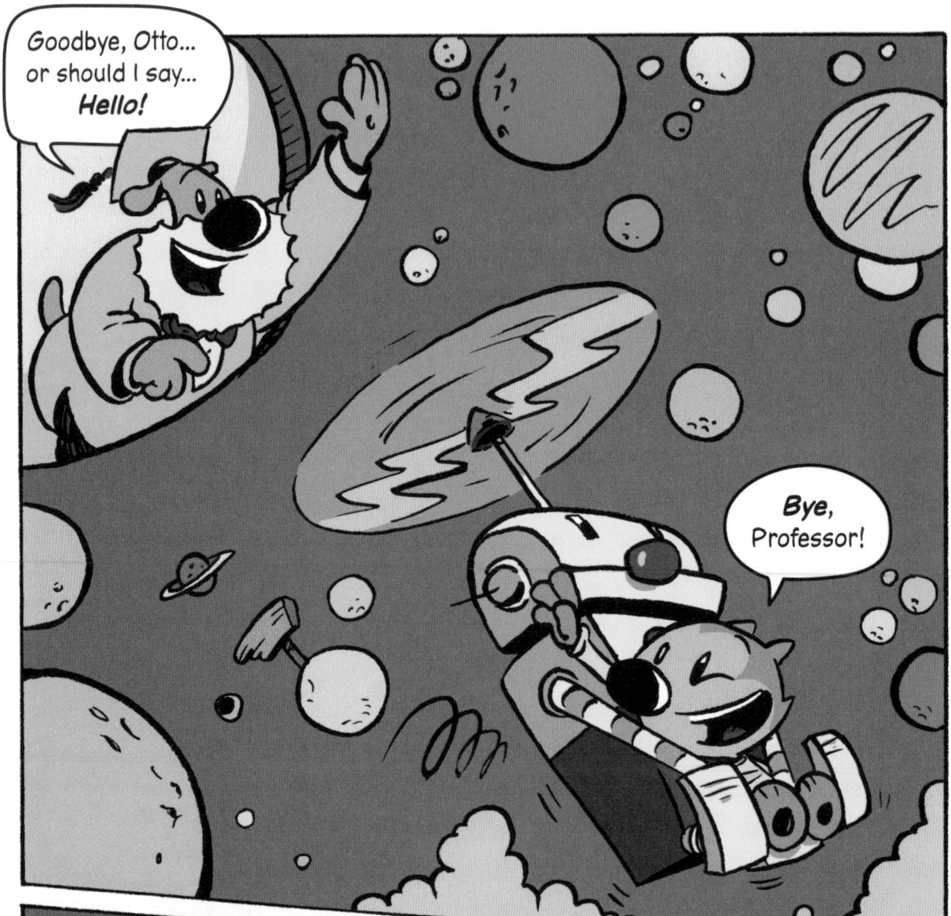
Goodbye, Otto... or should I say... **Hello!**
Bye, Professor!

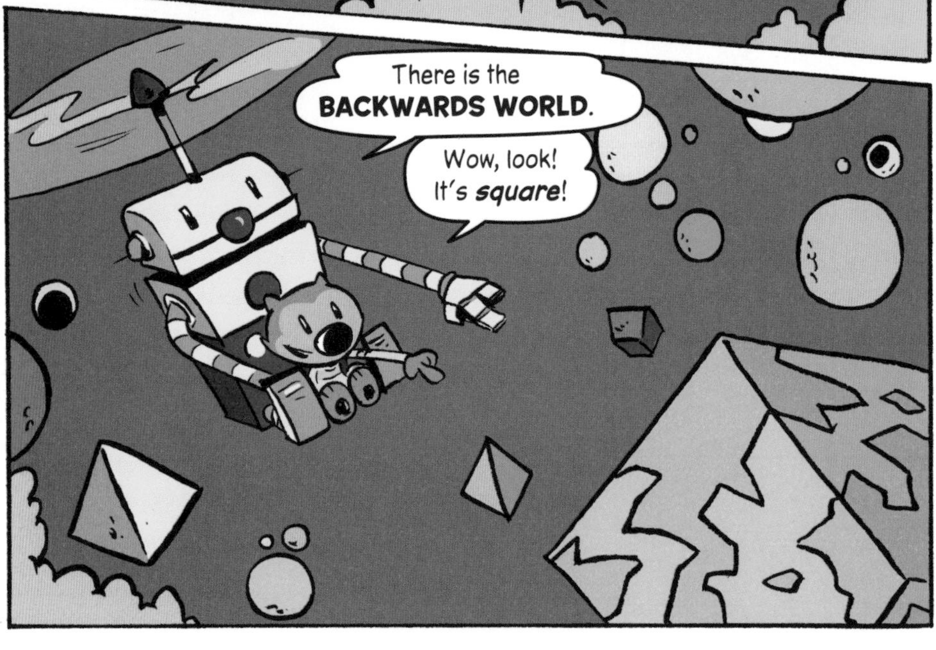
There is the **BACKWARDS WORLD**.
Wow, look! It's ***square***!

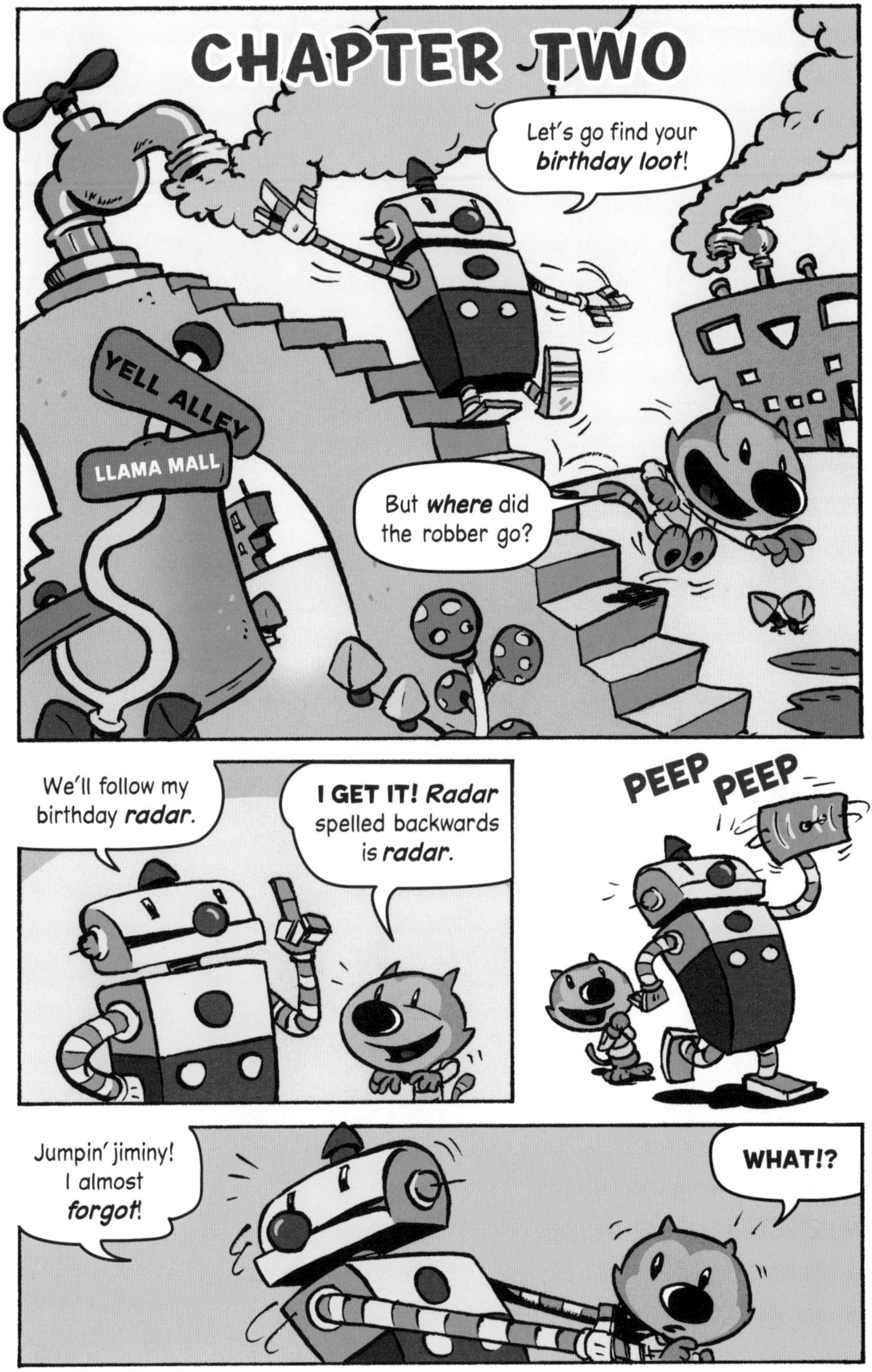
CHAPTER TWO
Let's go find your *birthday loot*!
YELL ALLEY
LLAMA MALL
But *where* did the robber go?
We'll follow my birthday *radar*.
I GET IT! *Radar* spelled backwards is *radar*.
PEEP PEEP
Jumpin' jiminy! I almost *forgot*!
WHAT!?

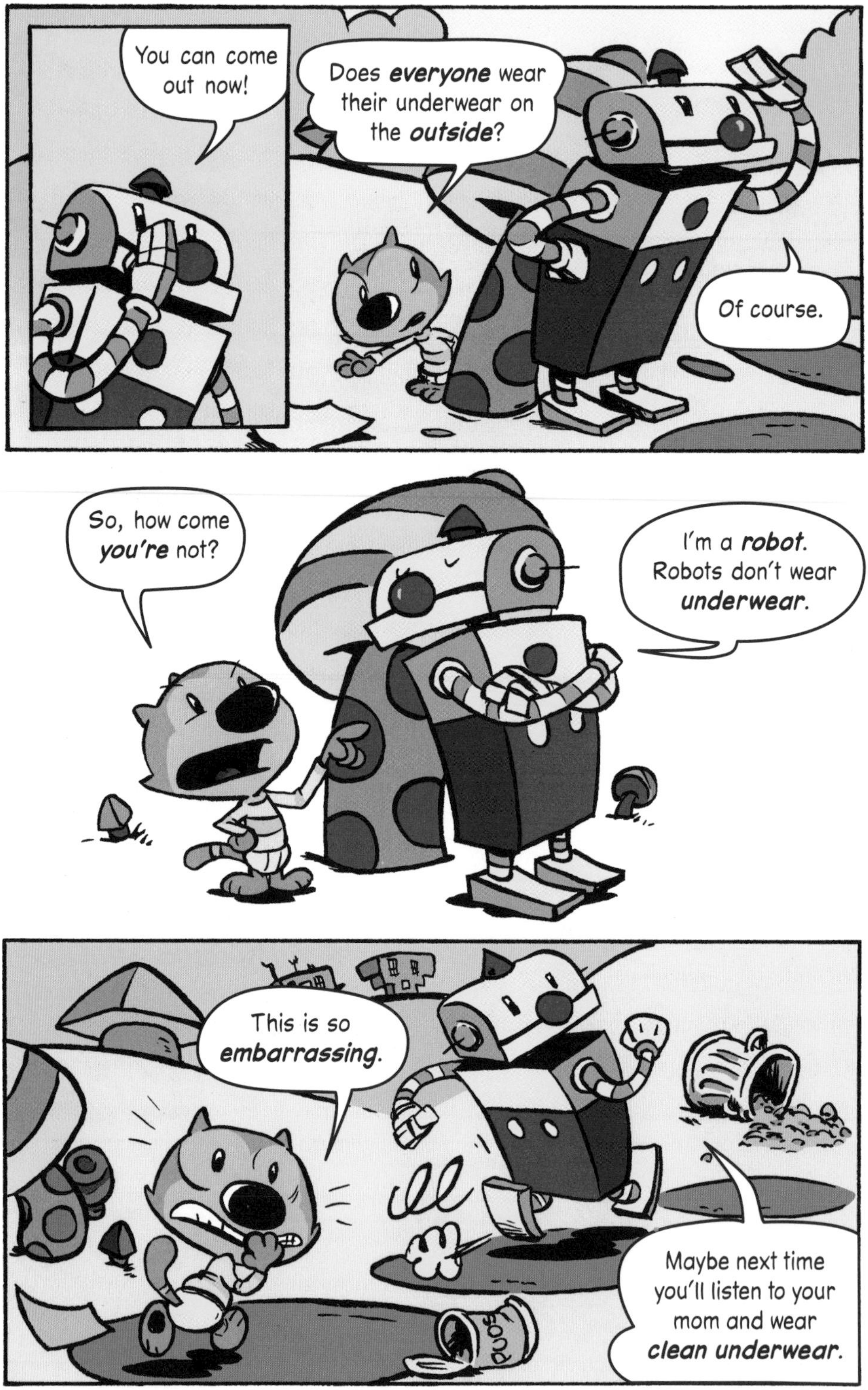
You can come out now!
Does *everyone* wear their underwear on the *outside*?
Of course.
So, how come *you're* not?
I'm a *robot*. Robots don't wear *underwear*.
This is so *embarrassing*.
Maybe next time you'll listen to your mom and wear *clean underwear*.

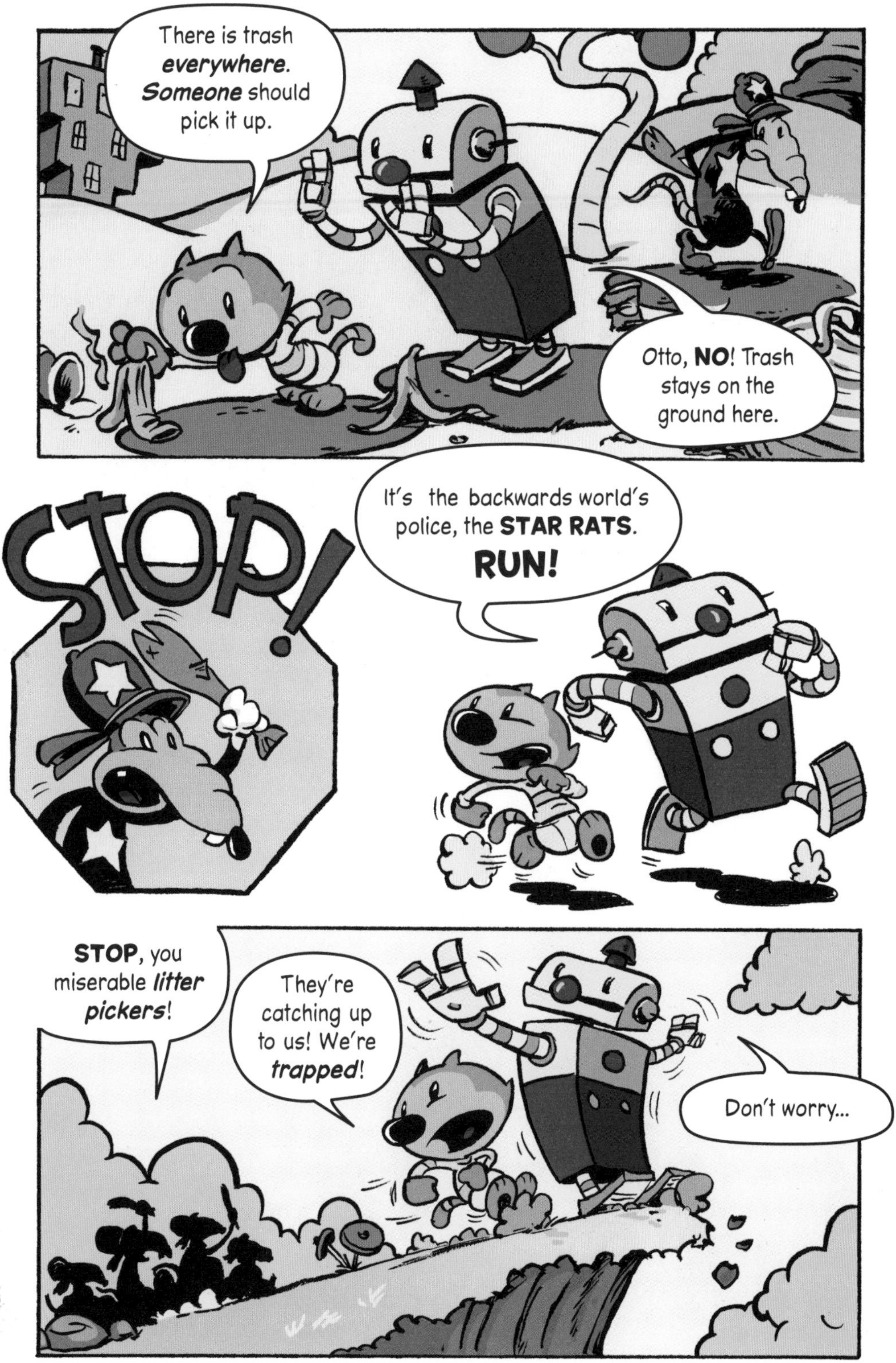
There is trash *everywhere.* *Someone* should pick it up.
Otto, **NO**! Trash stays on the ground here.
STOP!
It's the backwards world's police, the **STAR RATS**. **RUN!**
STOP, you miserable ***litter pickers***!
They're catching up to us! We're *trapped*!
Don't worry...

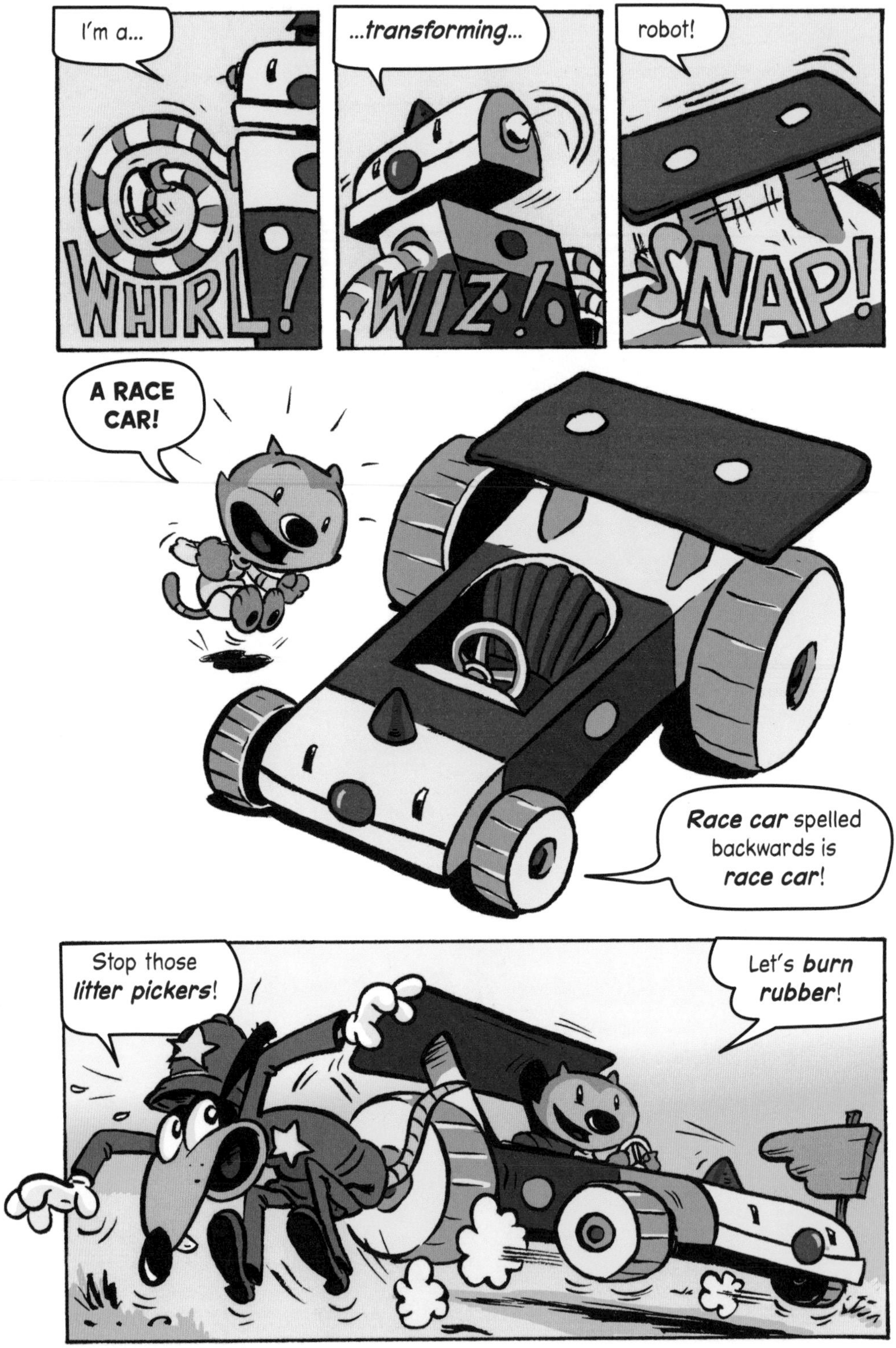

I'm a...
WHIRL!
...transforming...
WIZ!
robot!
SNAP!
A RACE CAR!
Race car spelled backwards is race car!
Stop those litter pickers!
Let's burn rubber!

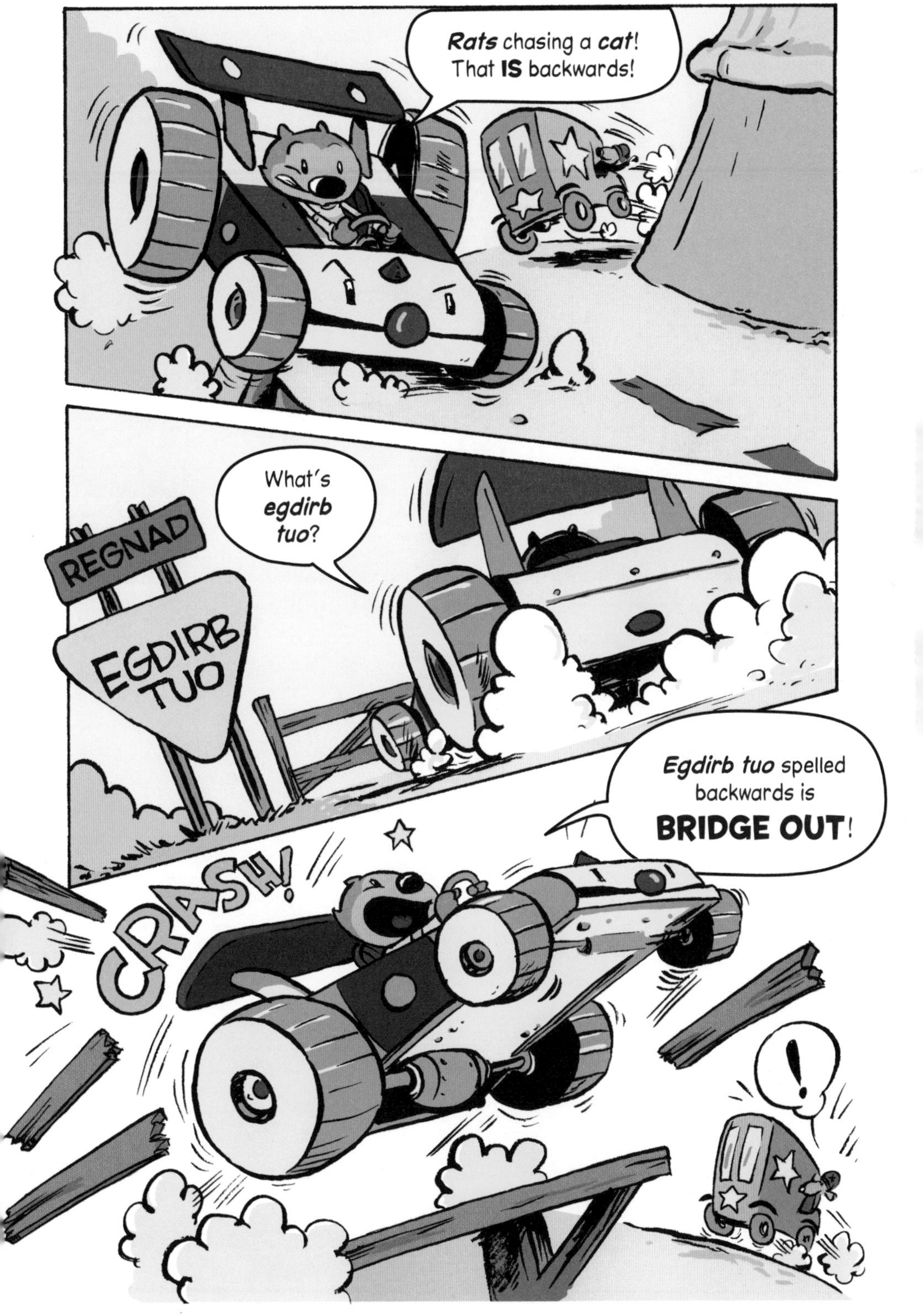

Rats chasing a *cat*! That **IS** backwards!
REGNAD
EGDIRB TUO
What's *egdirb tuo*?
Egdirb tuo spelled backwards is **BRIDGE OUT**!
CRASH!
!

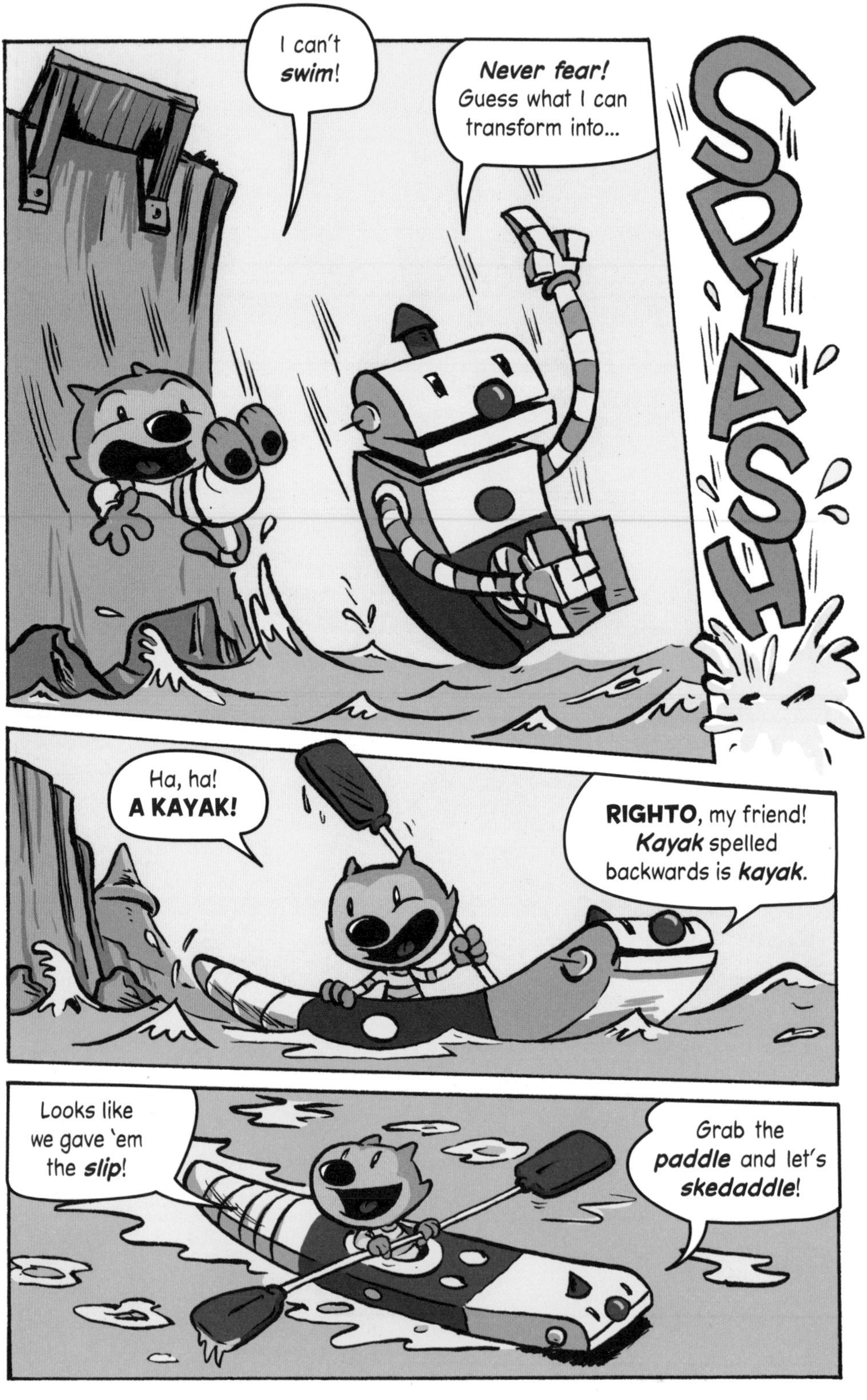
I can't *swim*!
Never fear! Guess what I can transform into...
SPLASH
Ha, ha! **A KAYAK!**
RIGHTO, my friend! *Kayak* spelled backwards is *kayak*.
Looks like we gave 'em the *slip*!
Grab the *paddle* and let's *skedaddle*!

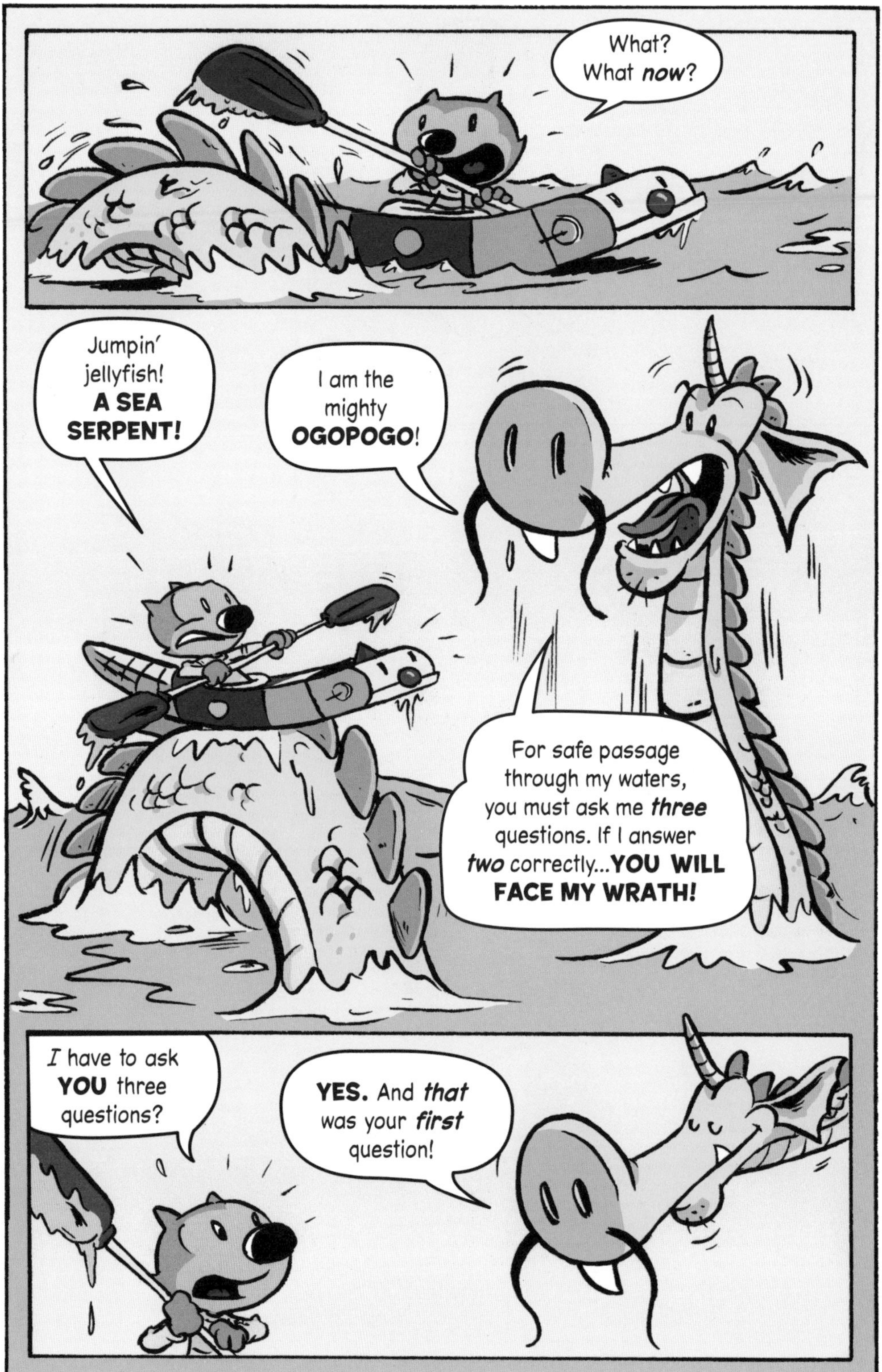
What? What *now*?
Jumpin' jellyfish! **A SEA SERPENT!**
I am the mighty **OGOPOGO**!
For safe passage through my waters, you must ask me *three* questions. If I answer *two* correctly...**YOU WILL FACE MY WRATH!**
I have to ask **YOU** three questions?
YES. And *that* was your *first* question!

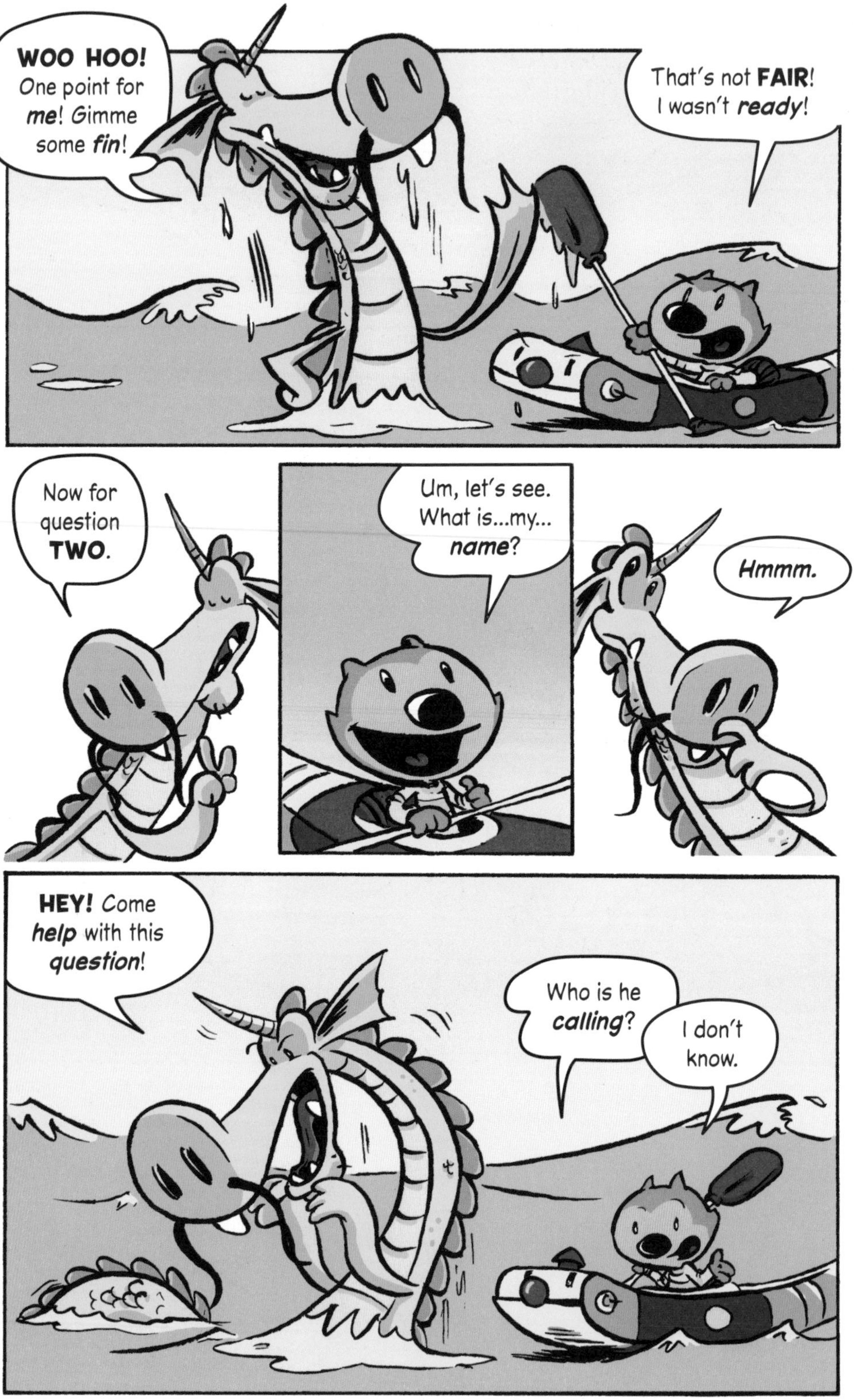
WOO HOO! One point for me! Gimme some fin!
That's not FAIR! I wasn't ready!
Now for question TWO.
Um, let's see. What is...my... name?
Hmmm.
HEY! Come help with this question!
Who is he calling?
I don't know.

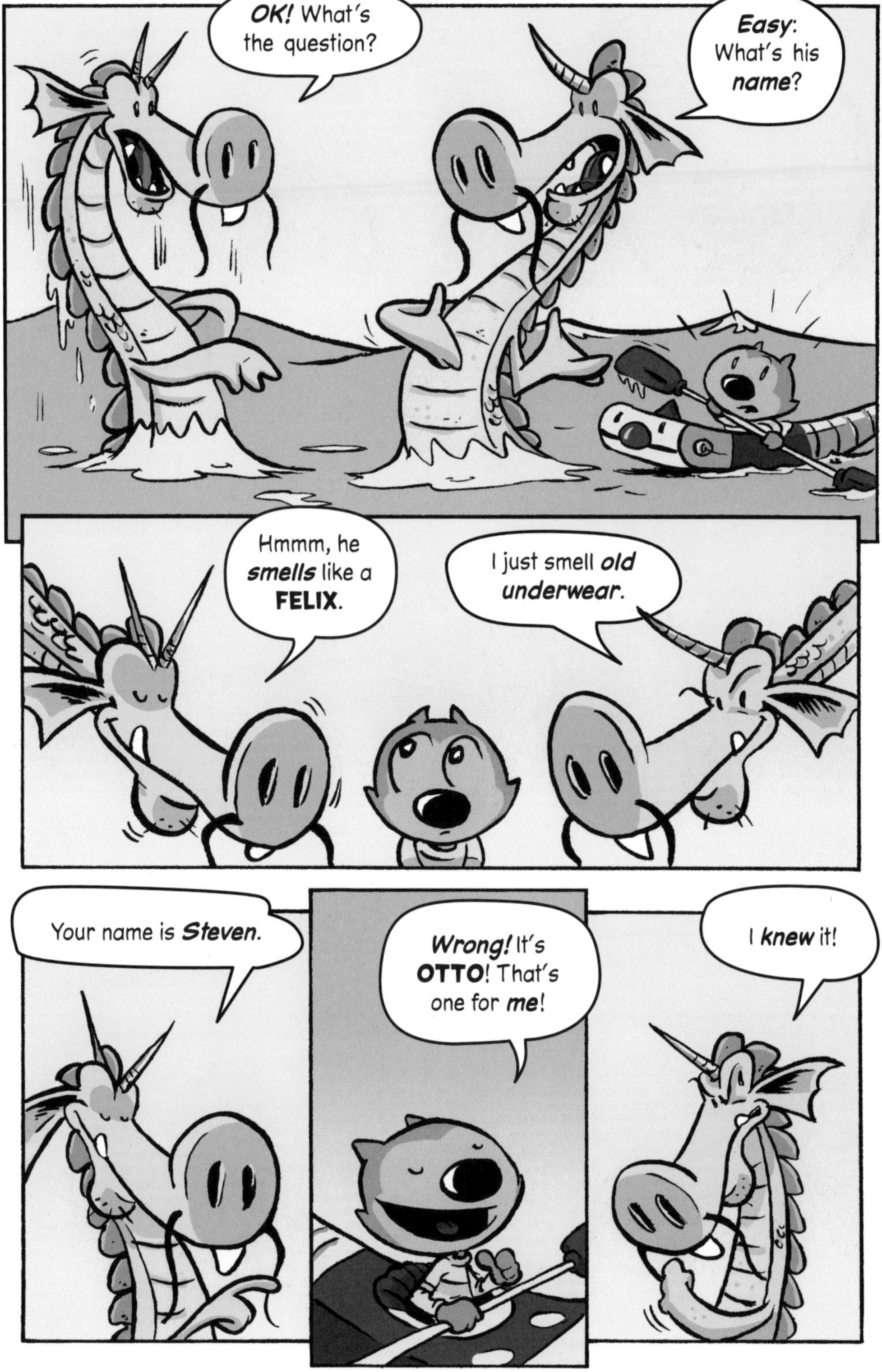
OK! What's the question?
Easy: What's his name?
Hmmm, he smells like a FELIX.
I just smell old underwear.
Your name is Steven.
Wrong! It's OTTO! That's one for me!
I knew it!

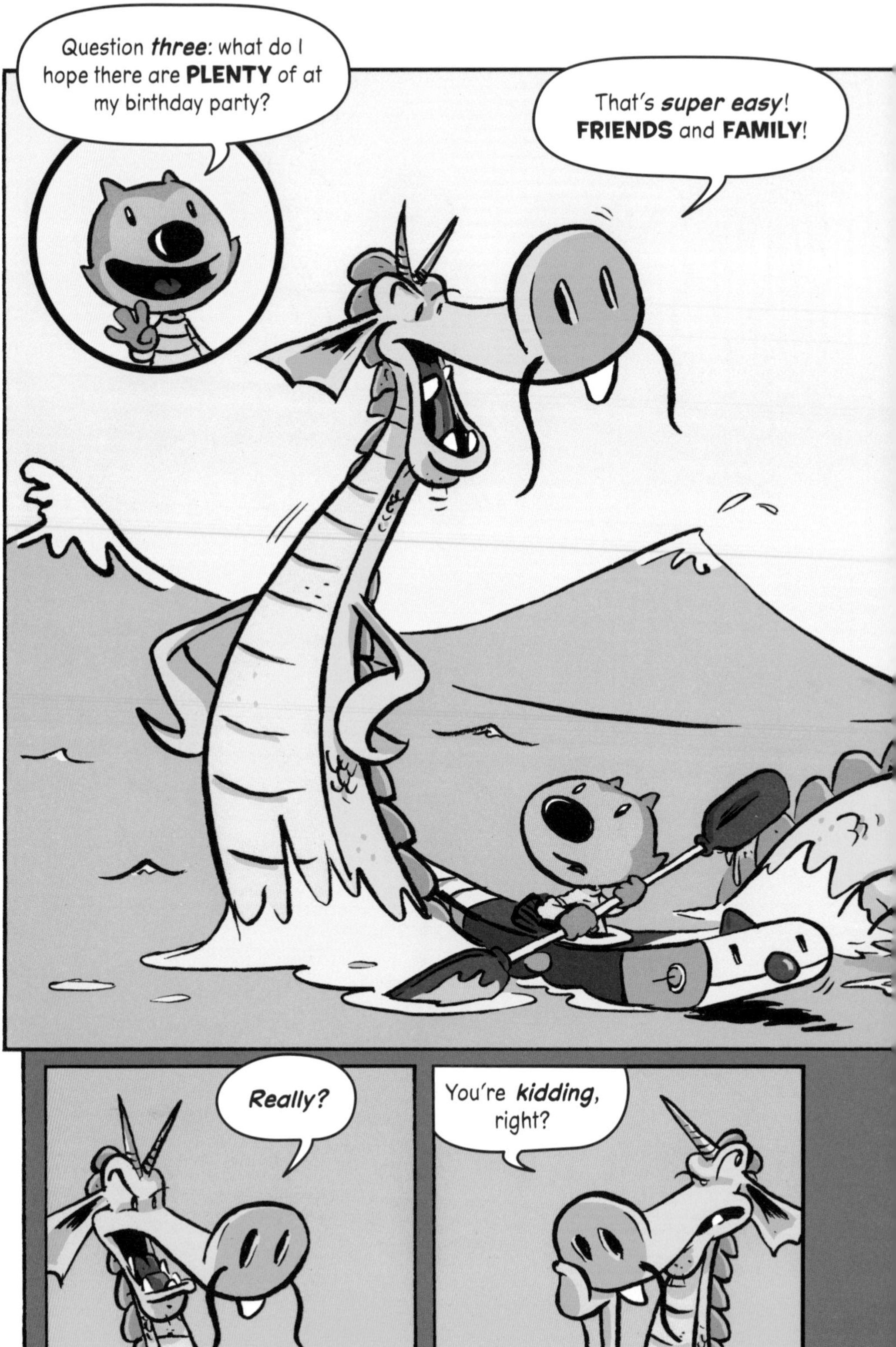
Question **three**: what do I hope there are **PLENTY** of at my birthday party?
That's **super easy**! **FRIENDS** and **FAMILY**!
Really?
You're **kidding**, right?

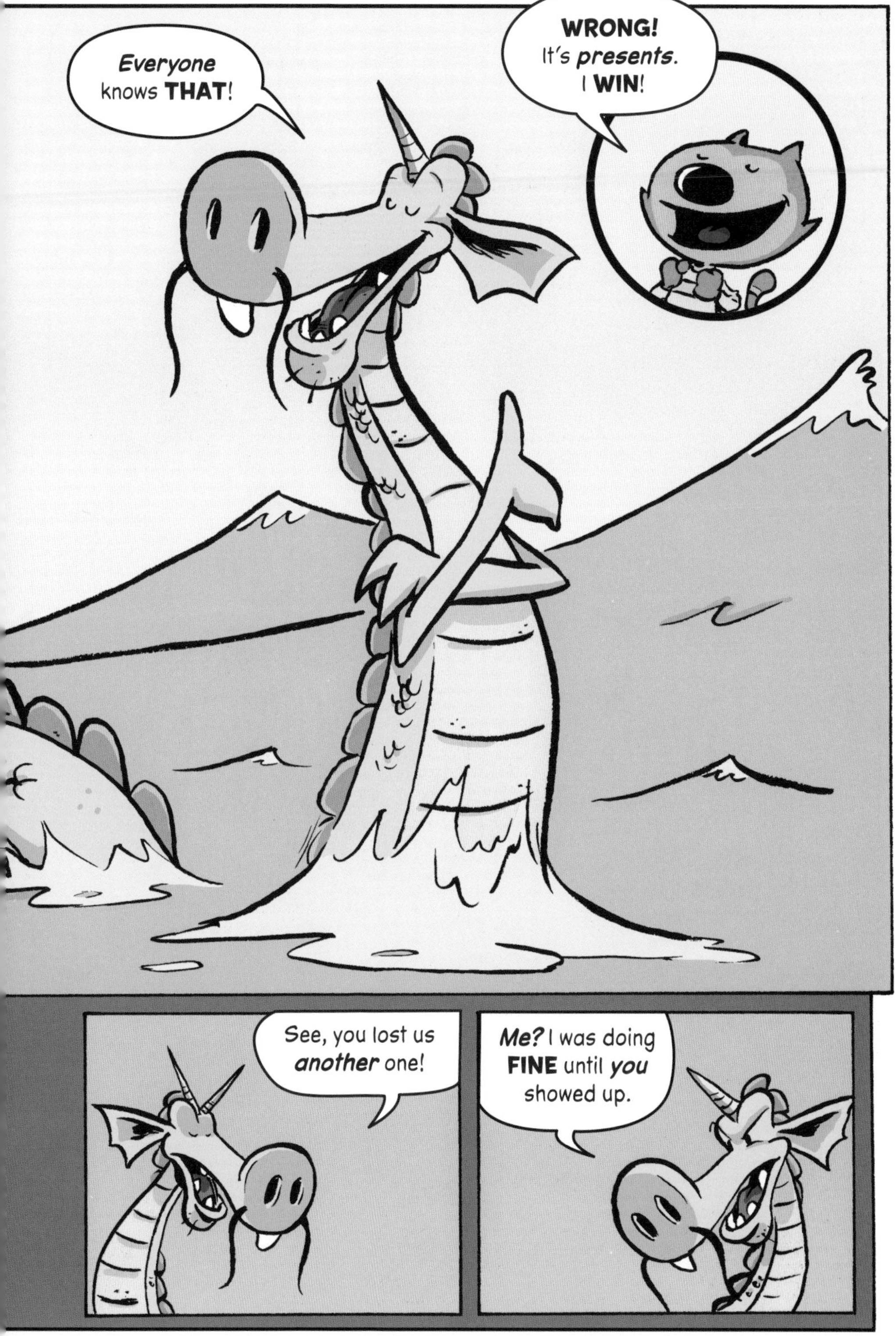
Everyone knows **THAT**!
WRONG! It's *presents.* I **WIN**!
See, you lost us *another* one!
Me? I was doing **FINE** until *you* showed up.

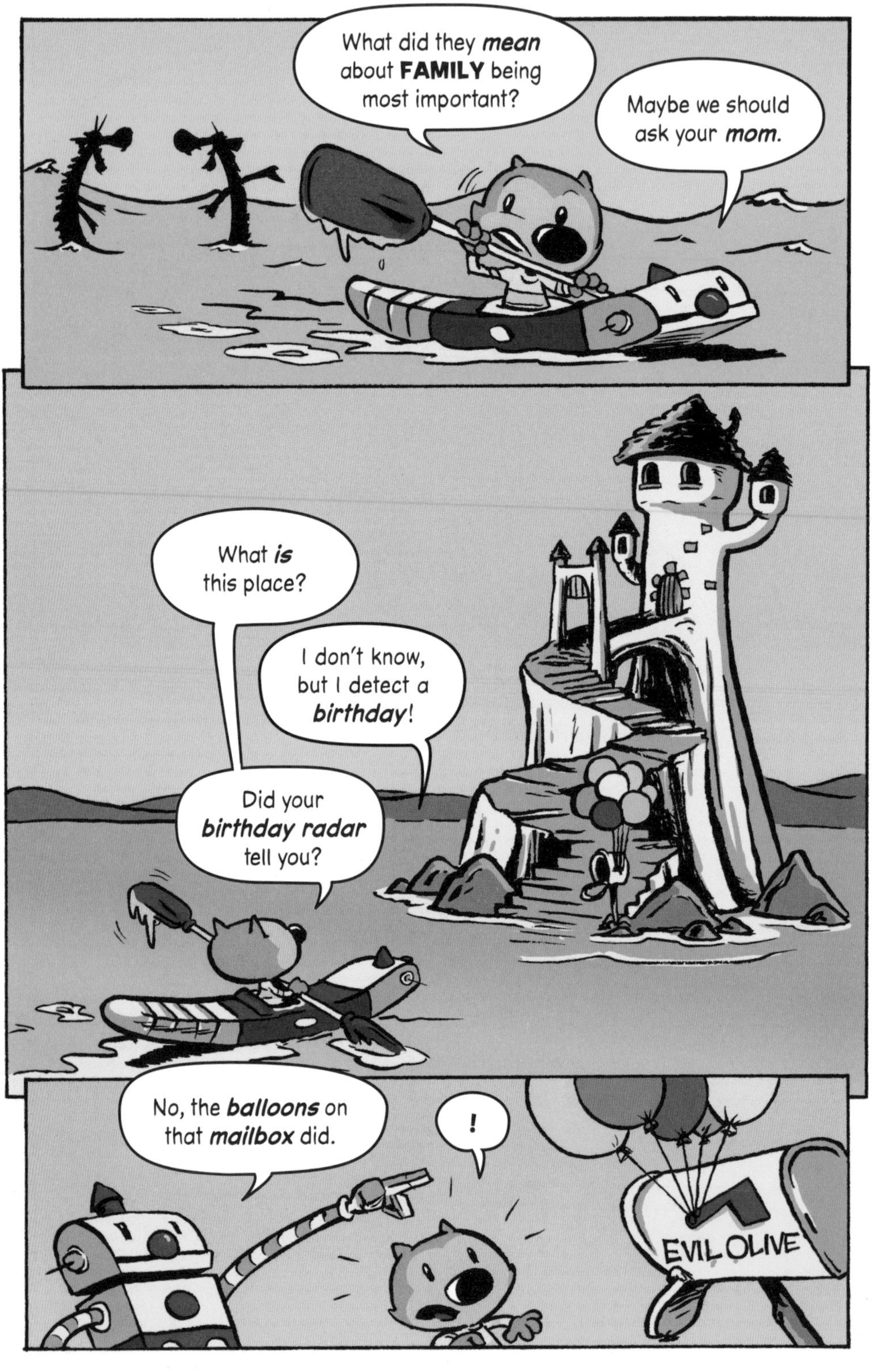
What did they *mean* about **FAMILY** being most important?
Maybe we should ask your *mom*.
What *is* this place?
I don't know, but I detect a *birthday*!
Did your *birthday radar* tell you?
No, the *balloons* on that *mailbox* did.
!
EVIL OLIVE

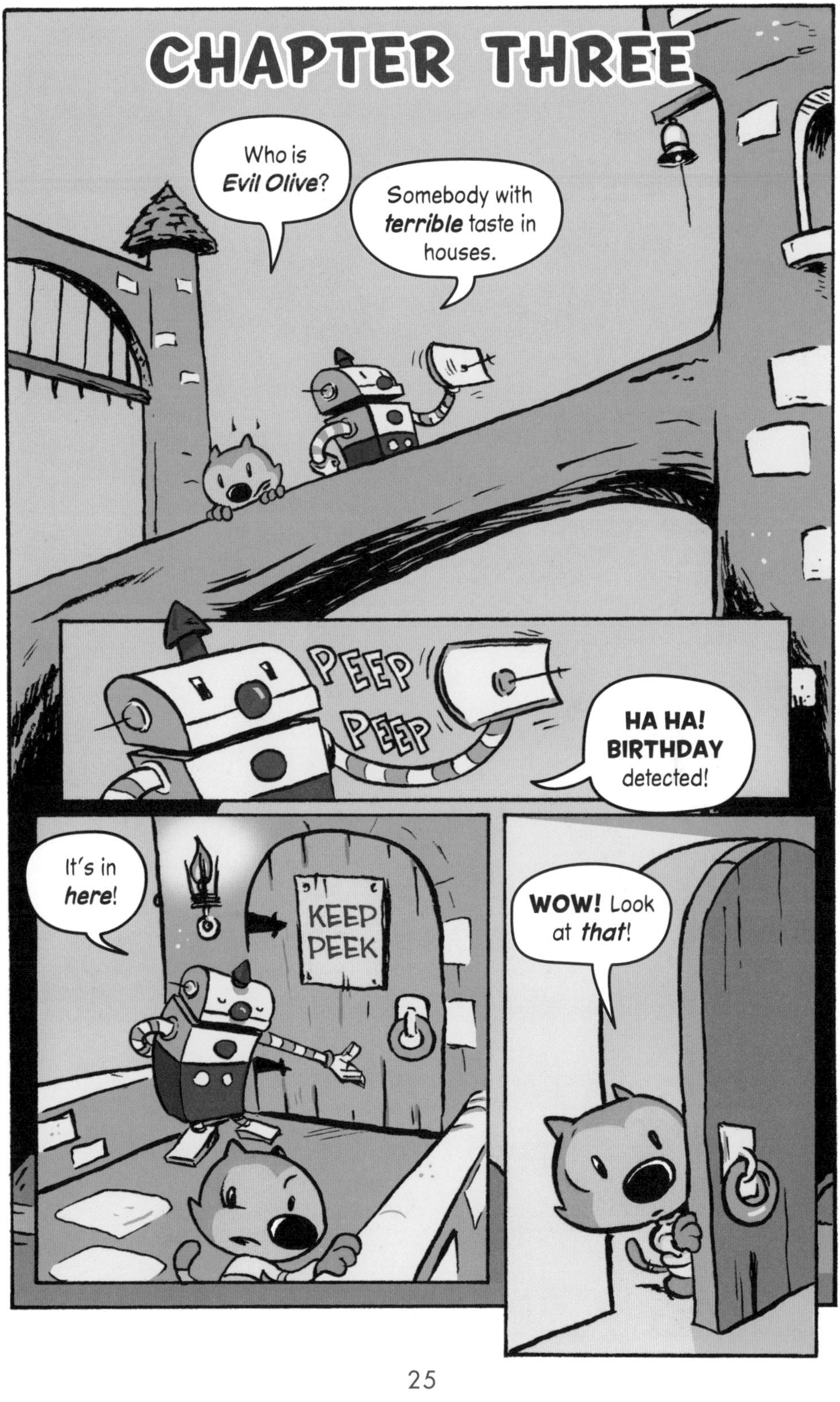
CHAPTER THREE
Who is *Evil Olive*?
Somebody with *terrible* taste in houses.
PEEP
PEEP
HA HA! BIRTHDAY detected!
It's in *here*!
KEEP PEEK
WOW! Look at *that*!

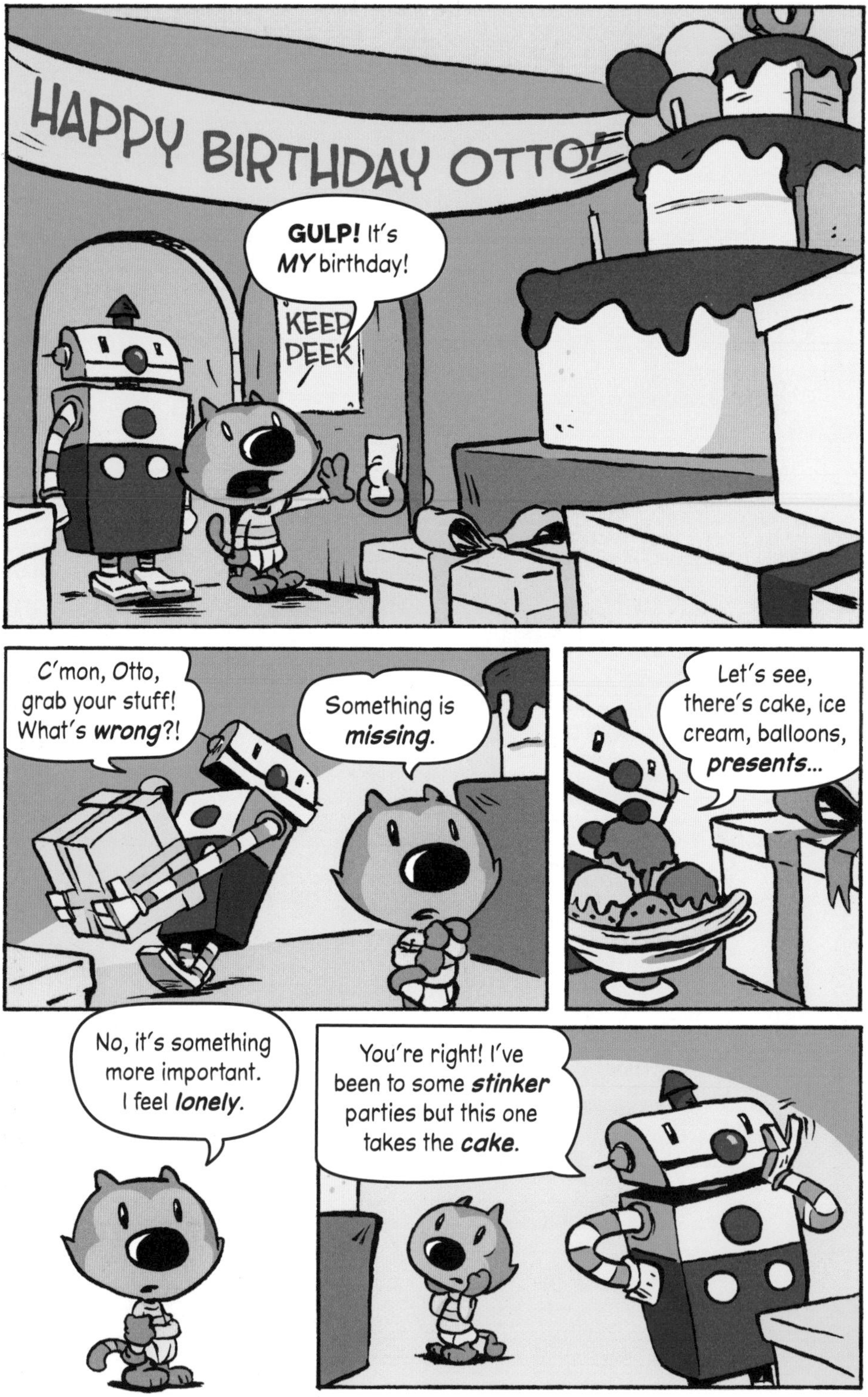
HAPPY BIRTHDAY OTTO!
GULP! It's *MY* birthday!
KEEP PEEK
C'mon, Otto, grab your stuff! What's ***wrong***?!
Something is ***missing***.
Let's see, there's cake, ice cream, balloons, ***presents***...
No, it's something more important. I feel ***lonely***.
You're right! I've been to some ***stinker*** parties but this one takes the ***cake***.

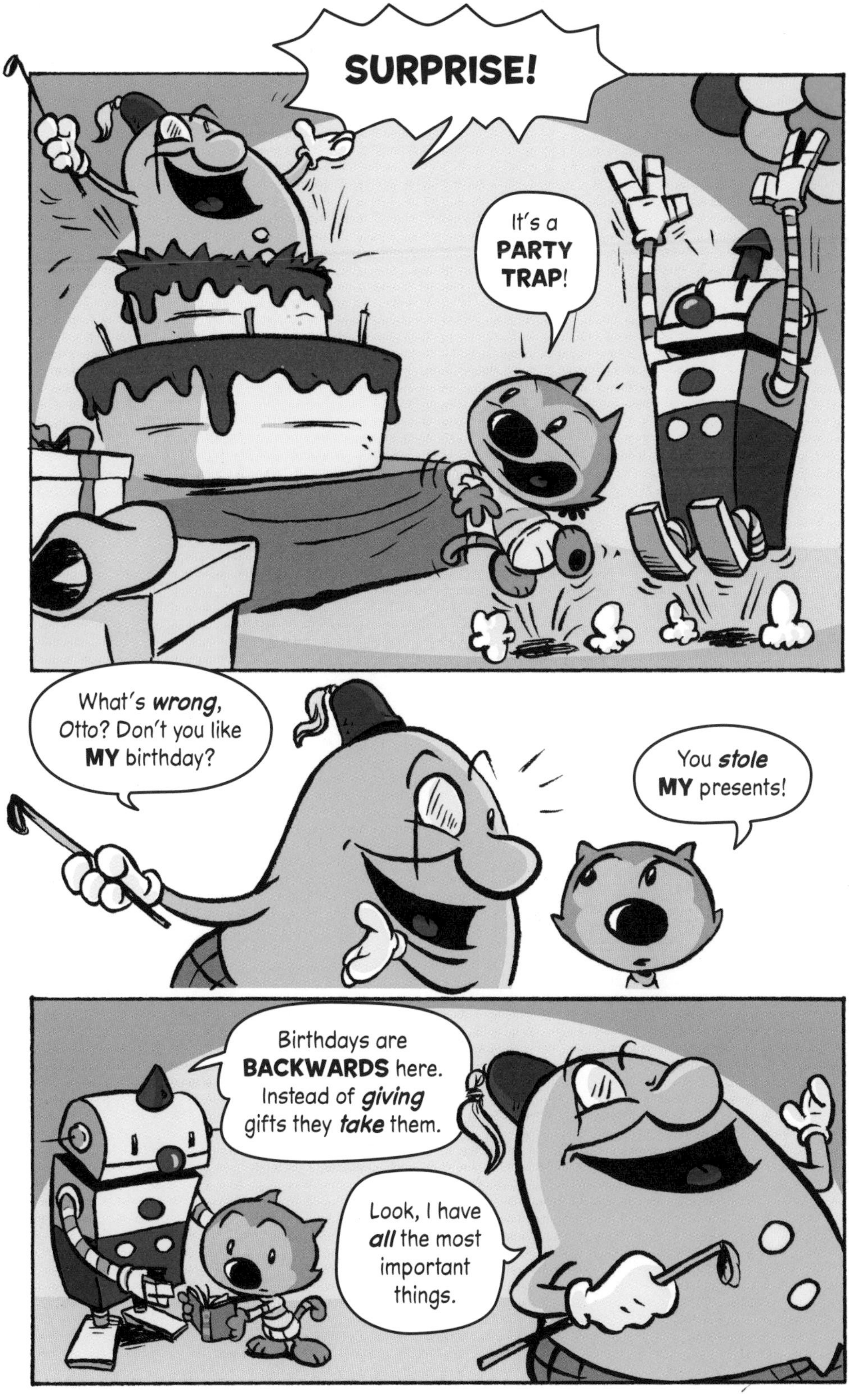
SURPRISE!
It's a PARTY TRAP!
What's *wrong*, Otto? Don't you like **MY** birthday?
You *stole* **MY** presents!
Birthdays are **BACKWARDS** here. Instead of *giving* gifts they *take* them.
Look, I have *all* the most important things.

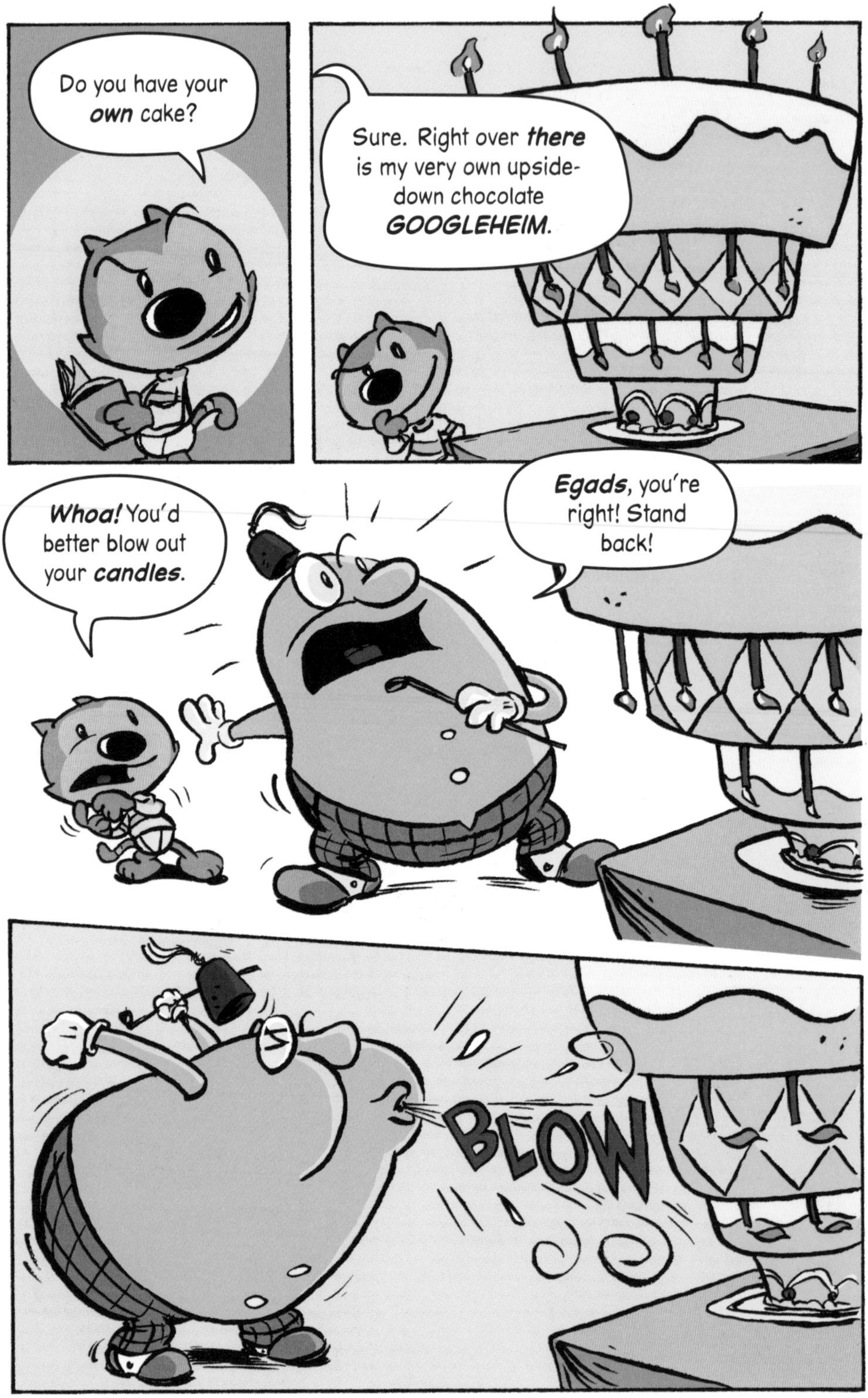
Do you have your *own* cake?
Sure. Right over *there* is my very own upside-down chocolate ***GOOGLEHEIM***.
Whoa! You'd better blow out your ***candles***.
Egads, you're right! Stand back!
BLOW

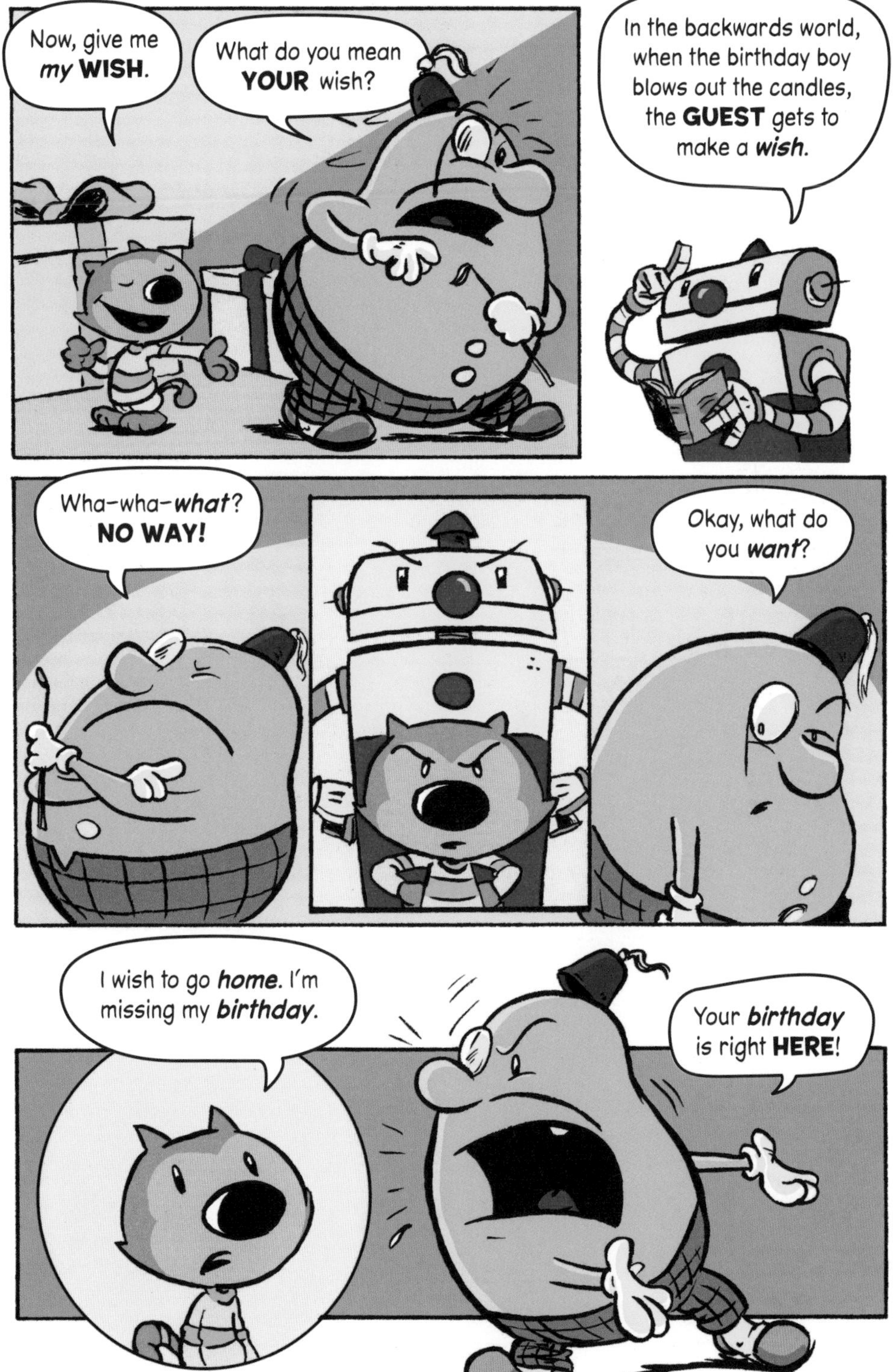
Now, give me *my* **WISH**.
What do you mean **YOUR** wish?
In the backwards world, when the birthday boy blows out the candles, the **GUEST** gets to make a ***wish***.
Wha-wha-***what***? **NO WAY!**
Okay, what do you ***want***?
I wish to go ***home***. I'm missing my ***birthday***.
Your ***birthday*** is right **HERE**!

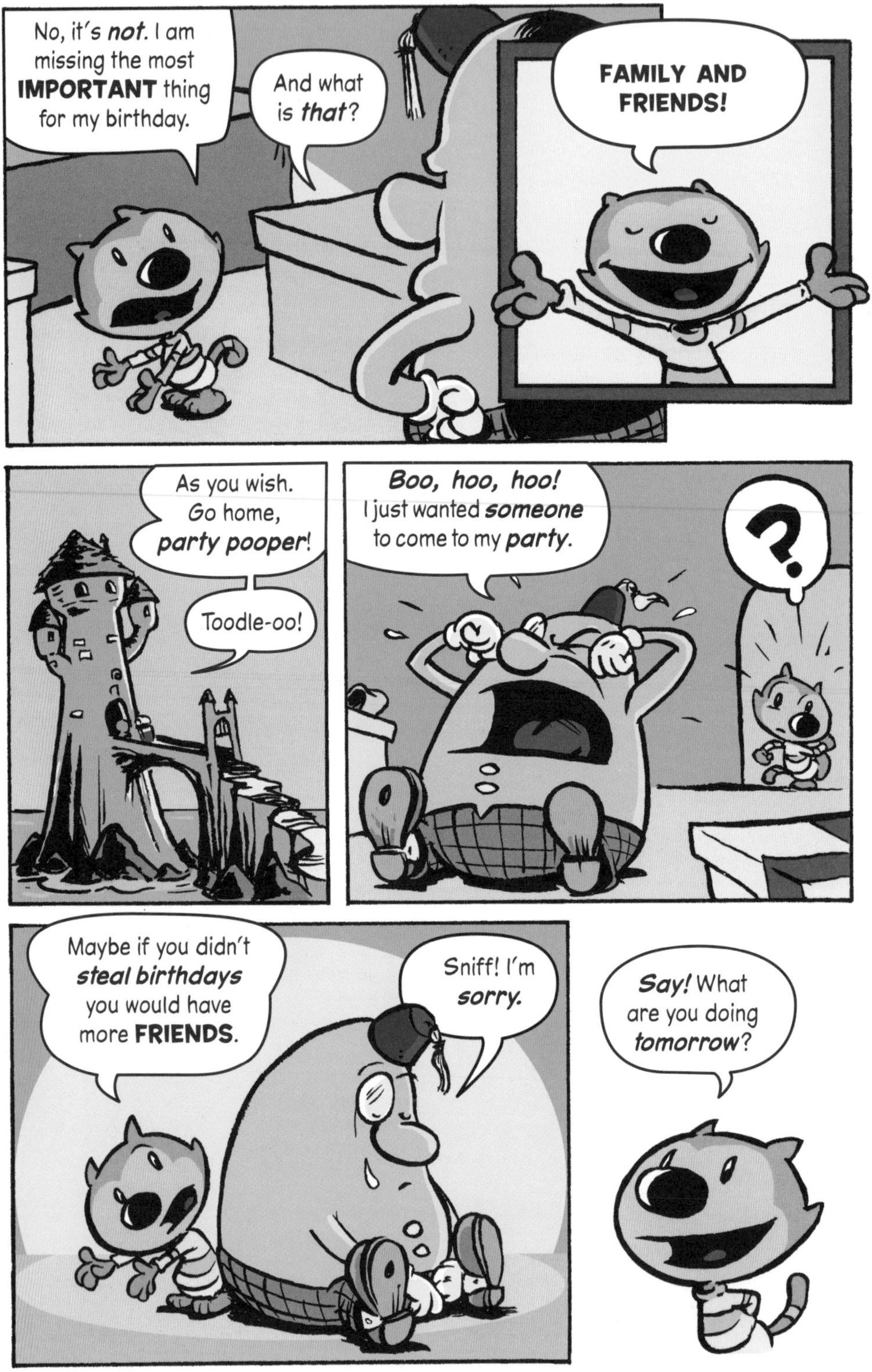
No, it's ***not.*** I am missing the most **IMPORTANT** thing for my birthday.
And what is ***that***?
FAMILY AND FRIENDS!
As you wish. Go home, ***party pooper***!
Toodle-oo!
Boo, hoo, hoo! I just wanted ***someone*** to come to my ***party***.
?
Maybe if you didn't ***steal birthdays*** you would have more **FRIENDS**.
Sniff! I'm ***sorry.***
Say! What are you doing ***tomorrow***?

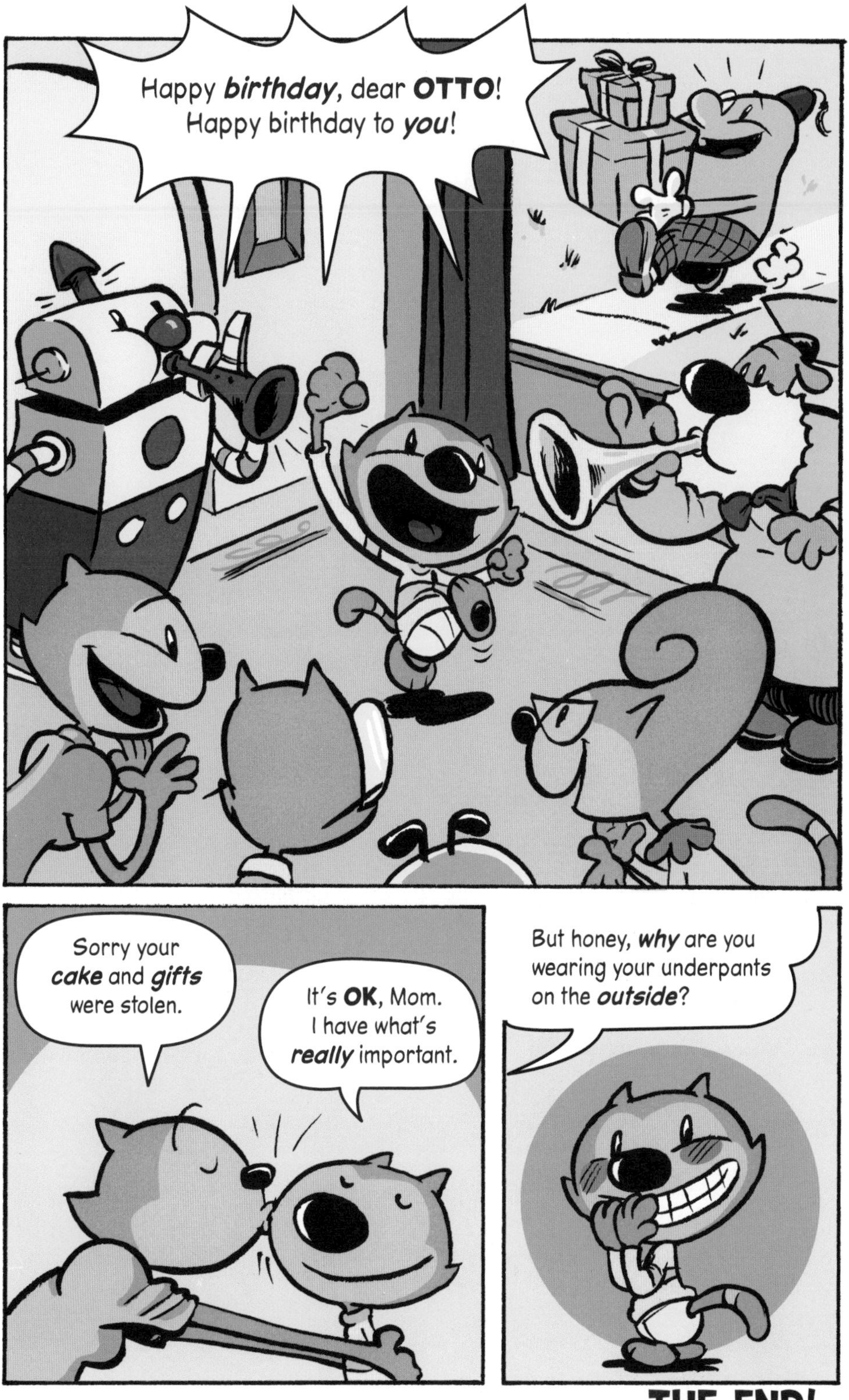
Happy *birthday*, dear **OTTO**! Happy birthday to *you*!
Sorry your *cake* and *gifts* were stolen.
It's **OK**, Mom. I have what's *really* important.
But honey, *why* are you wearing your underpants on the *outside*?

THE END!

ABOUT THE AUTHORS

FRANK CAMMUSO, who wrote and drew Otto's adventure, is the author of the graphic novel series *Knights of the Lunch Table*, a middle school version of King Arthur and his knights. His latest series, *The Misadventures of Salem Hyde*, is about a fun-loving, seemingly average kid who happens to be a witch. His writing has appeared in *The New Yorker*, *The New York Times*, *The Village Voice*, and *Slate*. **JAY LYNCH**, also a cartoonist, has helped create some of Topps Chewing Gum's most popular humor products, such as *Wacky Packages* and *Garbage Pail Kids*. Frank and Jay collaborated on the original TOON Book, *Otto's Orange Day*, which *School Library Journal* named a "Best New Book" and described as "a page-turner that beginning readers will likely wear out from dangerously high levels of enjoyment."

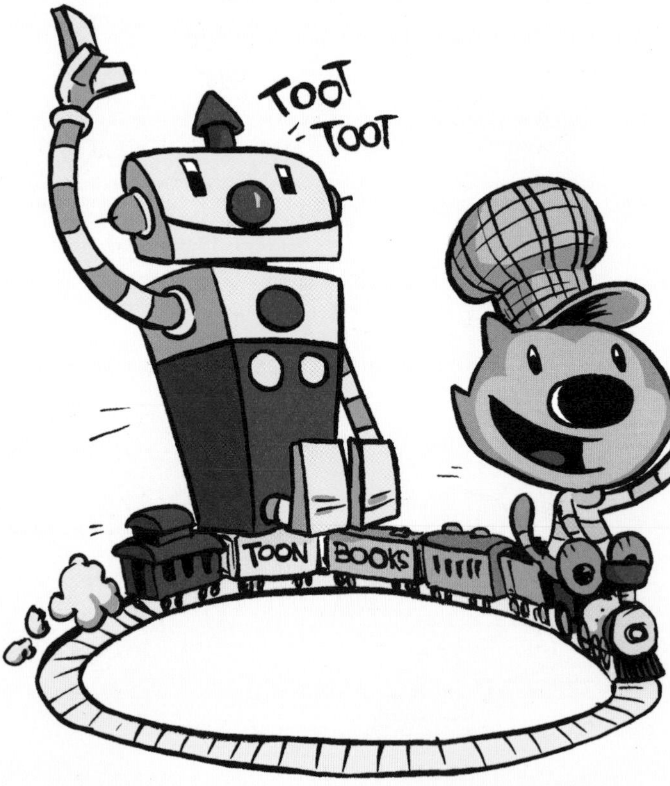
TOOT
TOOT
TOON
BOOKS

HOW TO "TOON INTO READING"

in a few simple steps:

Our goal is to get kids reading—and we know kids LOVE comics. We publish award-winning early readers in comics form for elementary and early middle school, and present them in three levels.

1 FIND THE RIGHT BOOK

Veteran teacher Cindy Rosado tells what makes a good book for beginning and struggling readers alike: "A vetted vocabulary, plenty of picture clues, repetition, and a clear and compelling story. Also, the book shouldn't be too easy—or the reader won't learn, but neither should it be too hard—or he or she may get discouraged."

The TOON INTO READING!™ program is designed for beginning readers and works wonders with reluctant readers.

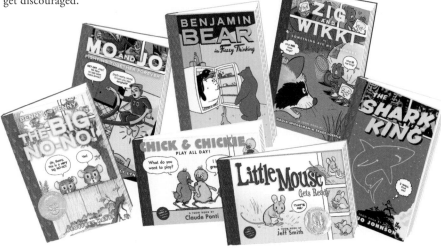

MO AND JO
FIGHTING TOGETHER FOREVER
BENJAMIN BEAR
in Fuzzy Thinking
ZIG AND WIKKI
NADJA SPIEGELMAN & TRADE LOEFFLER
BENNY AND PENNY
THE BIG NO-NO!
Oh, Benny, this is a very big NO-NO!
Yes!
GEOFFREY HAYES
CHICK & CHICKIE
PLAY ALL DAY!
What do you want to play?
A TOON BOOK BY
Claude Ponti
Little Mouse Gets Ready
THAT'S ME!
A TOON BOOK BY
Jeff Smith
THE SHARK KING

2 TAKE TIME WITH SILENT PANELS

Comics use panels to mark time, and silent panels count. Look and "read" even when there are no words. Often, humor is all in the timing!

KNOCK! KNOCK!
TRICK OR TREAT!

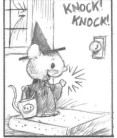

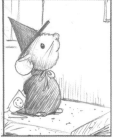

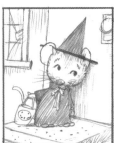

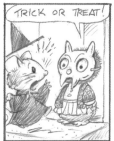

3 GUIDE YOUNG READERS

What works?
Keep your fingertip <u>below</u> the character that is speaking.

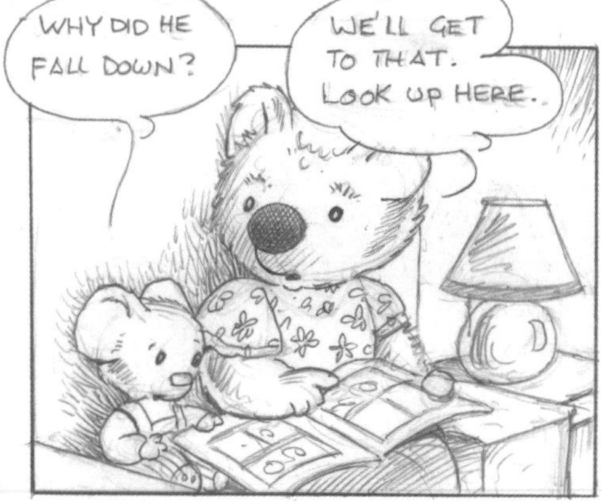
WHY DID HE FALL DOWN?
WE'LL GET TO THAT. LOOK UP HERE.

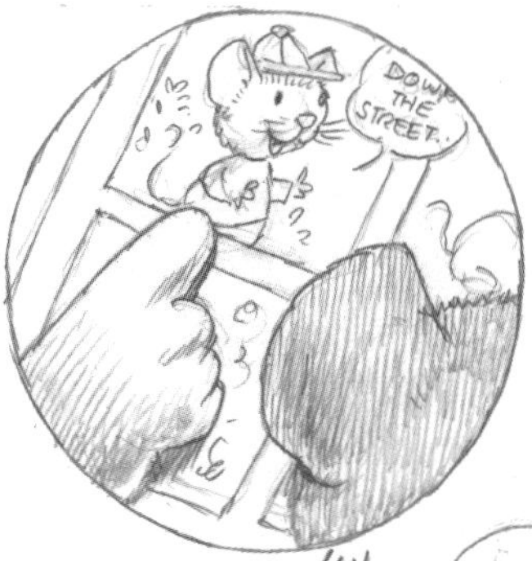

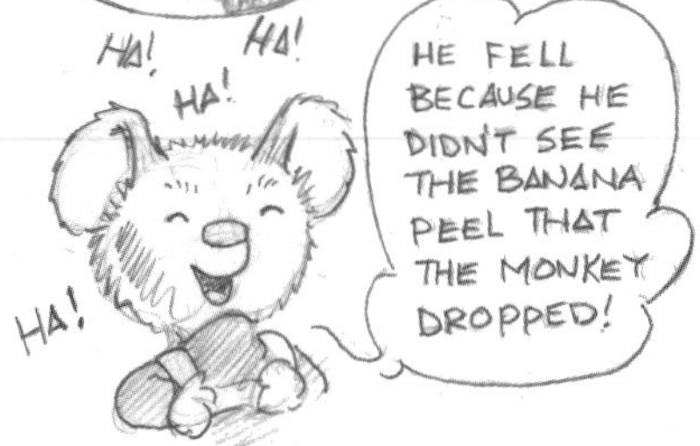
HA! HA! HA! HA!
HE FELL BECAUSE HE DIDN'T SEE THE BANANA PEEL THAT THE MONKEY DROPPED!

4 LET THE PICTURES TELL THE STORY

In a comic, you can often read the story even if you don't know all the words. Encourage young readers to tell you what's happening based on the facial expressions and body language.

5 GET OUT THE CRAYONS

Kids see the hand of the author in a comic and it makes them want to tell their own stories. Encourage them to talk, write and draw!

Get kids talking, and you'll be surprised at how perceptive they are about pictures.

6 LET THEM GUESS

Comics provide a large amount of context for the words, so let young readers make informed guesses, and don't over-correct. In this panel, the artist shows a pirate ship, two pirate hats, and two pirate flags the first time the word "PIRATE" is introduced.

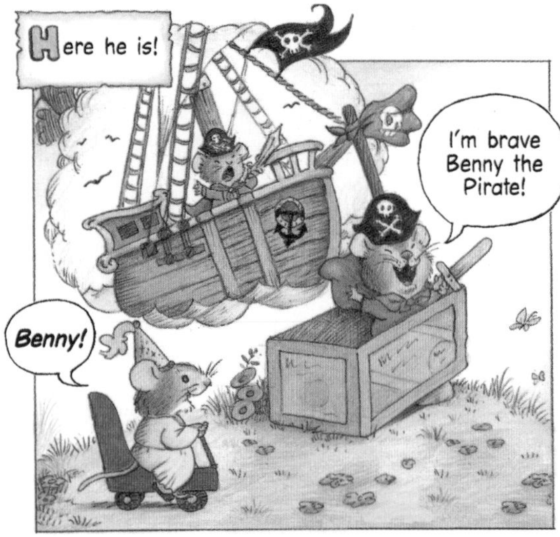
Here he is!
I'm brave Benny the Pirate!
Benny!